WHERE ARE MY CHILDREN?!

L. A. DAVIS

ABSOLUTE AUTHOR PUBLISHING HOUSE
New Orleans, LA

Absolute Author
Publishing House

WHERE ARE MY CHILDREN?!
Copyright © 2019 by L. A. Davis
Published 2019 by Absolute Author Publishing House

Line Editor: Dr. Melissa Caudle
Copy Editor: Erin N. Wright
Cover Graphic: elite cover on Instagram
Illustrations: alisalaheldinkrar on Instagram
Section Graphics: Free Graphics
Author Photograph: Darnley D. Davis

Library of Congress Cataloging-in-Publication Data
Davis, L. A.

ISBN: 978-1-7337182-5-7
Where Are My Children?!/L. A. Davis
    p. cm.
      1.   Fiction   2. Hurricane
            0 1 2 3 4 5 6 7 8 9

Printed in the United States of America

SPECIAL THANKS

Special thank you to Mrs. Mary Perry for your support.

L. A. DAVIS

DEDICATION

This book is dedicated to every ancestor whose blood was soaked into the soil during the Transatlantic Slave Trade. To those who entered the belly of slave ships and were cast into the ocean from the shores of Africa, to the shores of the Americas and beyond. May you never be judged by the choices you had to make. May you never be judged by the choices you couldn't make. May your souls forever rest in power as you rest in paradise.

I dedicate this book to those worldwide whose love and compassion rose above hate and bigotry to help those in need in the Caribbean and the United States during hurricane season 2017.

I dedicate this book to the people of the Caribbean for their resiliency after hurricanes Irma, Jose, and Maria.

I dedicate this book to the people of the United States Virgin Islands. We have shown the same resiliency as our ancestors before us. May we never let that die and may God continue to bless the Emeralds of the Sea.

L. A. DAVIS

TABLE OF CONTENTS

FOREWORD

By Anita Davis

As a broadcaster, I was on the air for both Hurricanes Hugo (1989) and Marilyn (1995), in addition to various others, smaller, but disruptive storms. Having gone months without electrical power, running water, mobile, landline telephones, and cable after those major storms, I have my island "legs." When I met L. A. Davis in 2014, I did not know she was working towards a Doctorate of Education (EdD) in Organizational Leadership/Development. The path to her goal was arduous, occupying several years of her life. She considered letting go of her dream several times. Through serendipity, she elicited the key to what she needed to do to proceed, and successfully defended her dissertation in 2017.

This entire experience awakened within her an intense desire to help others in similar straits. She founded *Pay it Forward USVI, Pay it Forward Caribbean, Virgin Islanders Business Directory* to enable helping hands and networking among the inspired. She is a *USVI Tourism Ambassador* and wrote her first book, *"So, you want to be a doctoral learner huh? Are you nuts?!: A short story of my difficult journey as an online doctoral learner, and some tips to help you succeed"* - a marvelous yet sometimes heartbreaking chronicle. I purchased that book because I wanted to support a local author, but it lit a fire in me. I offered to review it, in hopes that others would find out what I did: that the only voice that matters is your own, and that we must keep ourselves open to all gifts, regardless of how they are packaged.

In September 2017, Dr. Davis' beloved island home was overtaken by two horrifying hurricanes with just days between them. Irma demolished St. Thomas, Water Island, and St. John. While Irma dealt quite a blow, their sister island of St. Croix was not as severely affected. As local officials and residents launched into the recovery phase, we were warned of a new danger - Hurricane Maria. On September 19, 2017, Hurricane Maria seemed intent on finishing off whatever Irma had left, and we were utterly lost. US Virgin Islanders are citizens of the United States of America, but beyond the Caribbean Sea, we were invisible to the public before, during, and after the storms. The unincorporated U.S. territory of the Virgin Islands (originally purchased from Denmark in 1917), barely registers on television weather maps. Our proximity to the U.S. Commonwealth of Puerto Rico, just forty miles West, rarely get us an honorable mention. The Office of the Governor struggled to mount assessment and search and rescue details and had already thrown out the lifeline to Federal officials in advance, and I cannot sugarcoat this as this was a humanitarian crisis.

Along with electricity, food, water, sanitation, medical care, and shelter, the need for communication was dire. Many mobile network towers were affected, and the aerial telephone, cable and fiber optic systems were obliterated. Our underground fiber optics survived unscathed, as did any power lines buried underground. Nonetheless, the majority of the islands' residents were in the dark literally and figuratively, with no way to communicate. Desperately, L. A. Davis took to social media to sift for information and share it as best as she could. Others were as frantic as she was for these treasures from home. She sought solace in memories of how she and her family survived previous tropical storms and hurricanes when she was a little girl. She recalled folk tales the adults in her life would tell to distract or thrill the children during such times.

As she kept vigil, the inspiration for her second book, "*Where Are My Children?!*" was born. For it was during the days and weeks after Irma and Maria as she tried to reach us, that she imagined a truth that might have been -- a truth that connected her to home. If you are from the USVI, you will find a certain familiarity within the pages of this book. If you are not, you will discover the power of a culture that has sustained a resilient people for centuries. And, everyone, regardless of origin the book will revel in the ongoing story of the African Diaspora as seen through the eyes of the grieving forgotten.

L. A. DAVIS

PROLOGUE

September 2017 is a year that I millions in the Caribbean and around the world will never forget. One Category 4 and two Category 5 Hurricanes came within weeks. They tried to wipe the entire Caribbean off the face of the earth. Hurricanes Irma, Jose, and Maria were vicious Cabo Verde tropical waves that bloomed into destruction. It was the first time I had ever seen hurricanes go up the Caribbean chain like a bowling ball trying to mow the islands down like pins as hard as they could.

The Hurricanes didn't hit every island directly, but they touched most in some way. Jamaica was the only island that escaped the season of dread, but in their history, they too have had their loss. Irma boiled through the Caribbean with a vengeance, Jose couldn't decide what to do, and Maria followed her sisters to make history. Whatever islands hurricane Irma missed; Maria tried to finish. Those bitches were angry. Angry at who? Angry, for what?

In the Virgin Islands, we have Hurricane Supplication Day which falls on the fourth Monday of July each year. My grandmother always called it *Pray Against Hurricane Day.*

I remember paying attention to the first weather pattern as soon as it popped up on the radar. There was something about her that left an unsettled feeling that would not leave my consciousness alone.

There are many things in my life that I never thought I would live to see. The World Trade Center brought to its knees, an

WHERE ARE MY CHILDREN?!

African American president, and two Category 5 hurricanes within weeks of each other trying to scrub the very existence of my island home off the face of this planet. I could never have imagined the massive destruction Irma would bring. I watched daily as the weather pattern crept closer and closer to the Caribbean and my island home. I spent time willing Irma by envisioning myself standing over her and blowing her back into the Atlantic Ocean. It was not to be. No amount of prayers was going to change her mind. She had unfinished business, a score to settle, and nothing was going to stop her.

Days before Hurricane Irma hit, I posted a warning on my social media page not to play with this storm. Irma had not made landfall anywhere, but I knew something ominous was coming. I take nothing away from the people in the direct path of Irma. I can't imagine the terror that resonated with the people dealing with those monsters. For those of us outside of those islands, it was agony. The emotional havoc those storms played on the people in the worldwide diaspora was almost unbearable. Hurricanes Irma, Jose, and Maria brought men to tears.

People were angry feeling that Puerto Rico got more news coverage than the USVI when Irma hit. I lost ten pounds and much sleep in a week. I felt guilty because I had my home, electricity, food, and no way to get any help home. I helped other groups on social media post messages of missing people to ease the mind of worried family members. I contacted our Congresswoman's office in Washington D.C. to find out if there was anything else that I could do. The gentleman who answered the phone told me to continue doing what I was doing on social media. It gave me a sense of purpose and kept my mind occupied. I wanted to collect food and clothing to send home. That would have fallen on deaf ears. Hurricane Harvey had displaced thousands of people who came to our small city for refuge. When Harvey hit, my family collected bags of clothing and food which I took to the local collection center. No one cared about Hurricane Irma or the Virgin Islands.

December 2017, after hurricanes Irma, Jose, and Maria retired into infamy, I watch via social media as St. Thomians as we are known on the island of St. Thomas, assembled in a park that was created to commemorate the abolition of slavery in the USVI on July 3rd, 1848, named The Emancipation Garden.

The Master of Ceremony with his beautiful, smooth, dark skin, his long locks tucked neatly into his tam, and his signature bright colored clothing introduced each musical number. Children and adults performed like there was no devastation. In the background, I saw trees with broken branches, but three things stood out that made me proud. The first one took me back to my favorite Christmas story. *How the Grinch Stole Christmas.* Even though the Grinch had stolen all the Christmas gifts, food, decorations, and the last crumb that was too small for a mouse, the villagers gathered outside. They realized that the true gift was in their hearts. With family and friends, they show this sentiment through singing.

Unfortunately, there was no Grinch in this story to give back what was stolen. Despite everything Hurricanes Irma and Maria had stolen, the people still came together to show gratitude and some form of normalcy. The second thing was seeing those who came out to support the performers. It made my heart smile to see the crowd clapping while some performers played instruments and others danced. The third thing was seeing our bandstand which has been in the garden since circa 1879. She has changed over the decades but she is still there. This structure is used for official ceremonies, celebrations, for tourists and locals alike to enjoy, community service to those in need and for anyone to admire while they sit in the park enjoying the sunshine and sea breeze from the waterfront.

Hurricanes Irma and Maria were no match for it. When I saw the canopy on my computer screen, I let out a sigh of relief. Seeing the bandstand when bigger and newer

structures were decimated, gave me a feeling of relief, pride, strength, and reassurance that everything was going to be ok. It perfectly represented the people who the Emancipation Garden was built to honor.

After Hurricanes Irma and Maria, I became fascinated with these juggernauts of fury. There were four major hurricanes that year. Harvey, a Category 4 Hurricane. Irma, a Category 5 Cabo Verde Hurricane. Jose, a Category 4 Cabo

Verde Hurricane, and Maria a Category 5 Cabo Verde Hurricane.

Harvey developed in the Gulf of Mexico, picking up steam while chugging towards the Texas coast and its surrounding cities. Harvey was two hundred miles across and dumped over fifty inches of rain. The National Weather Service had to add a new color to the radar map to identify the amount of water this Hurricane produced. Harvey hit the coast of Texas three times before his remnants moved to Louisiana. Sixty-eight souls were lost with one hundred and fifty, to one hundred and eighty billion dollars' worth of damage.

My Childhood Experience with Hurricanes

Growing up as a child we were ignorant to the seriousness of hurricanes; to us, they were fun. They were nothing like they are today. There were devastating hurricanes in recorded history, but I never saw hurricanes coming so frequently and with such intensity. Although hurricanes are a nuisance, we prepared for them as a normal part of island life. Schools, stores, and all manner of businesses would close as they prepared for each passing storm. Windows would be boarded up; chicken coops would be secured, and dogs would run under the bed.

On the island, we have no underground gas lines. We have various sizes of tall, cylinders that hold propane. Before any hurricane approached, all propane tanks would be shut off by turning its circular valve. After the storm passed and everyone felt it was safe to go outside, boards on windows were removed. In some cases, the boards were removed by the winds with the nails still embedded in the wall. Neighbors

WHERE ARE MY CHILDREN?!

would come outside to check on each other and assess damage in the community and to their property.

In our home, we expected flooding with each storm. My grandmother always told us that when you see cockroaches flying, it meant rain was coming, and those cockroaches didn't make a liar out of her. We spent many a night as children screaming under our sheets with our legs and arms being used as tent poles as we heard the buzzing and whirring of cockroach wings.

Indoor flooding was a fun time for us. We would play around in the water and run away from "donkey spiders" (Tarantulas) that were looking for a dry place of refuge and respite. After a couple of days of the frightening winds that sounded like massive whistles or roaring beasts, the rain beating the house in tempo, and things beating up against the windows like they were daring us to come outside and fight, my grandmother would take a broom and sweep the water out of our home. Another nuisance we had to deal with after hurricanes were mosquitos. We always found fun in the things my grandmother did and smoking out the house was one of the best times.

Not only do mosquitoes sting, spread disease, and get fat off blood, but the smallest mosquito can deprive you of sleep due to their unharmonious singing. My grandmother had an old metal bin that she always used to smoke the house out from mosquitoes. She would find an old brown paper bag. She would put the paper in the bottom of the shallow bin and place dried twigs on it. After striking a match and laying it against the brown paper, she would click her tongue as if she was encouraging the flame to bloom. As the brown paper ignited, it would cause the twigs to ember. The twigs would produce a thin layer of gray smoke that would have us coughing and laughing while suffocating any mosquito who dared to enter the house. We would go to bed and have the most incredible night's sleep.

Depending on the severity of the hurricane, it would take several days for the electricity to come on, but we still had to eat. If people chose to cook inside, then gas tanks would be turned back on. Some preferred to use an ancient style of cooking called a coal pot that must be used outside. You could choose to put the pot directly onto the hot coals, or you could put a grill over the coals and set the pot on it. It is a part of my culture that I hope never dies. My grandmother had a gas stove that I only saw her use a few times during my childhood. Her coal pot was the prized possession that she used daily.

Sometimes we used charcoal briquets commonly used in the United States. Other times if we had it, we would use coal made from natural wood. The limbs of trees would be buried and burned underground for days, producing black, chunks of burnt wood. You haven't had a true Virgin Islands childhood until you've stepped on a hot piece of coal.

WHERE ARE MY CHILDREN?!

Each island in the Caribbean thinks they are better than the other; not only in cuisine but also in skin tone, hair texture, and length. Slave masters perpetuated this myth to cause division among black people and others. It was meant to make them feel superior, and black people inferior. Centuries later, we have not stopped this hateful rhetoric.

Although the loss of homes was not easy to deal with, and there were vast differences within the people, those forms of vanity didn't matter during times of disaster. Islanders always came together in such natural events. I never grew up seeing selfishness amongst Virgin Islanders or people of the Caribbean when it came to hurricanes. If it existed, we were shielded from it. I pray that never changes.

Global Warming and Climate Change

I believe that human beings are born with good hearts that become tainted by our experiences. Due to life and the human condition, we become greedy, hateful, jealous, envious, vengeful, and murderous. Men believe they have the right to pillage, rape and place entire nations into bondage. Other men feel they have the right to subject certain ethnic groups to genocide. These men are often wealthy leaders and individuals who choose their prey wisely due to the color of their skin, their gender, their religious beliefs, their crimes, their class, their intellect, or just for the hell of it.

Men can sit around a table, design the most diabolical instruments of destruction and death in secret. They kill the guilty while using collateral damage as an excuse when the innocent is killed. They label these instruments of death as justice. How do you explain one man having the power to order grown men to kill or enslave the innocent by the millions? Simple answer, we give them the power. We do not pay close attention, we have apathy, and by the time we have figured it out, it is too late. We take back our power when we pay attention, band together, and say, "No more."

I have the utmost respect for nature. We cannot control her. She has all the power, and she does not take orders from men. Over the years there has become an increase of knowledge on global warming and climate change; I believe in both. Some people don't believe in this phenomenon, and that is okay. Ignorance does not make it untrue. Summers are becoming hotter and more prolonged. Winters are becoming shorter and warmer in some parts of the world while in others, winters are becoming longer and colder.

Areas of this planet that should to be frozen solid are now melting, killing entire ecosystems, releasing deadly bacteria, and leading wildlife to slow starvation. While one part of the country is burning up with fire and heat waves, another part of the country is flooding.

Although I do have concern for the conditions of our planet, I never allow such things to bother me. Whether we put systems in place to help the earth heal or not, nature has a way of getting things into balance. Human beings cannot destroy her. If she has to shake rattle and roll, huff, and puff to blow your house down, vomit her heat, stretch her oceans beyond its boundaries to do it, that is what she will do. She makes no apologies, and she takes no prisoners. All you can do is get out of her way.

Taking all of this into account, what if changes in the weather patterns have nothing to do with global warming, climate change or nature trying to get herself into balance? What if weather patterns have more to do with the mistakes of our past?

WHERE ARE MY CHILDREN?!

Childhood Superstitions

Growing up, we all had that one monster or old wives' tales that scared us. For some, it was The Green lady, The Gray Man, The Bogey man, La Diablesse, Bloody Mary, La Llorona, The Candyman, The Lamia, and superstitious sayings such as, "Step on a crack break your mother's back." We have all heard them. My culture is full of fun superstitions that frightened me as a child. My grandmother told me never to pick up a penny from a crossroad. She never told me why, but all these years later in 2018, I found out that there is a demon that can be summoned at the crossroad that you must give pennies too as an offering. Even if what my grandmother told me isn't true, I live by three crossroads. If I see a penny, I just keep it moving.

On St. Croix, they have the Goat-foot Woman. In St. Thomas we have our beloved Cowfoot Woman and the Jumbie.

As children, we would break open little brown pods that held red seeds with a black spot we call Jumbie beads. Some wore them around their necks as chains. The beads were supposed to keep these invisible beings away.

L. A. DAVIS

Walking in the cemetery was something done briskly, or we would run with eyes straight ahead not daring to look at any graves. I was told to never point at a grave or the dead person would haunt me. As a child, my father busted that superstition by pointing at graves while we were walking the street between two cemeteries after I said innocently, "Daddy, don't point at the graves, the dead people goin' haunt you." My father took his pointer finger and pointed at each grave as he made a sound with his tongue perched between his lips.

My father is still around decades later never being visited by the dead. Now that I am an adult, superstitions are just that. I give each superstition its due respect because it is my personal belief that all superstitions, no matter how bizarre,

WHERE ARE MY CHILDREN?!

or scary they seem, they came from somewhere. I am going to use my imagination, and culture of superstition to tell this story of fury, and a revenge that will never be satisfied.

L. A. DAVIS

CHAPTER 1

The Genesis of Hurricane Names

Hurricanes have a history of being named after saints. In the 1890s a British born meteorologist who moved to Australia is credited with giving names to weather disturbances. He named disturbances in Greek alphabetical order. He also named some after Greek and Roman Characters, names of politicians he was not fond of, and women he admired. In the 1940s the United States Armed Forces used the phonetic alphabet to name storms. In 1950 that changed when three hurricanes caused confusion with internal communication.

The first hurricane given a name was Hurricane Able in 1950. In 1953, hurricanes began to be named after women. This was met with controversy since the storms were given names as adjectives for a woman's behavior. Alice became the first human named tropical storm, with Barbara becoming the first human named hurricane. In 1979, men's names were added to the hurricane database.

There are six lists of twenty-one hurricane names that circulate. Names are alternated by gender in alphabetical order. If a storm is retired, another name is added to the list to take its place. If a hurricane season becomes extraordinarily active and all twenty-one names are used, the list goes to the Greek alphabet. The last time this happened was in 2005; the season that hurricane Katrina wreaked havoc on New Orleans.

WHERE ARE MY CHILDREN?!

The Atlantic region has its list of six names, and the Eastern Northern Pacific region has its list of six names. Names are English, Spanish, or French are used on this side of the hemisphere. Why am I giving information on names of tropical storms and hurricanes you might ask? For individuals in the western hemisphere, names of hurricanes matter. To Mother Africa, it doesn't.

Cabo Verde

Cabo Verde also known as The Cape Verde islands are located approximately four hundred miles West of Senegal and made up of ten islands. Barlavento (Windward) group are Santo Antão, São Vicente, Santa Luzia, São Nicolau, Sal, and Boa Vista. The islands in the Sotavento (Leeward) group are Maio, Santiago, Fogo, and Brava. Santa Luzia is the only uninhabited island.

Not all hurricanes form off the West coast of Africa, but when they do, they are female, and Mother Africa does not care about their name. All Mother Africa cares about is finding her children. Her children are the souls of slaves sold off her coasts and Madagascar. They have been gone for centuries, and she will not stop looking for them. Mother Africa has been grieving since the Transatlantic Slave Trade began; she is still recovering.

Centuries after the Transatlantic Slave Trade ended there have been hundreds of hurricanes that have set records. The worst Cabo Verde Hurricane in recorded history created devastation to Barbados, Martinique, and Sint Eustatius with twenty-two thousand souls lost between October 10th to October 16th, 1780. The year 2005 hurricane season produced the most Cabo Verde

17

hurricanes with four hitting the Americas. The 1914 hurricane season produced the least number of Atlantic hurricanes.

Although most hurricanes are cast off the Cabo Verde islands, in 2015, Hurricane Fred barreled through Cabo Verde. The only other known storm to hit the Cabo Verde was September 12th, 1892. Hurricane Five formed affecting Cabo Verde without making direct landfall. She disappeared over the Atlantic Ocean on September 23rd, 1892.

Resting in Power

In 2015, Hurricane Danny formed approximately eight hundred- and twenty-five-miles Southwest of Cabo Verde. She hit the Caribbean as a Category 3 Hurricane. Hurricane season 2016 was a busier hurricane season. There were fifteen storms, seven became hurricanes and four were major. Hurricane Alex formed in the Northeastern Atlantic in January. This was unusual because hurricane season usually starts in June and ends in November.

Tropical storms Bonnie, Colin, Fiona, Ian, Julia, Karl, Lisa, and Hurricanes Danielle, Earl Gaston, Hermine Matthew, Nicole, and Hurricane Otto finished the season. Hurricane Matthew was a very unusual storm. Though many North Atlantic Hurricanes form off Cabo Verde, she developed somewhere in the middle of the ocean between the Americas and Cabo Verde. Matthew went past the Windward Islands, and then made a sharp northerly turn cutting through Haiti, the Dominican Republic, and Cuba. She went back into the Atlantic Ocean, picked up strength and slammed into the Bahamas and then Florida.

WHERE ARE MY CHILDREN?!

Mother Africa went into a long slumber and came out of hibernation on August 26th, 2017 with fury. She had been resting in her power when a terrible nightmare awakened her. A nightmare about her missing children. The children whom she has been searching for centuries. She heard then crying for her.

During the 2017 hurricane season, the United States was in a year of a new presidential administration and the United States was in chaos. The country seemed to be taking a turn back to one of the darkest times in its history. It was beginning to affect the world. Relationships between friends and family were being severed due to politics. Marriages dissolved because some could not understand how their partner could support the person they couldn't. Family and friends were unwilling to sit down and enjoy a football game because of their differing views. Thanksgiving and Christmas dinners were avoided because there was so much division. Some gathered together with the promise to not discuss politics at the table. If some felt the need to discuss it, those that wanted no parts of it would go to different rooms in the house. Racial, ethnic, and religious tensions from the past that were hidden and not buried, were beginning to bubble to the surface like oil. It needed to happen so that it could be weeded out. The souls of Mother Africa's children began to cry out to her from the continent of the Americas, the Caribbean Sea, from the Atlantic Ocean, and from within Mother Africa's boundaries.

Wailing women, prayer warriors from Mother Africa's descendants, and prayer from others who went into intercession could also be heard as their prayers went out into the atmosphere. What no one knew, was that Mother

L. A. DAVIS

Africa heard it, and she was about to get involved in a powerful way.

Hurricane Harvey intervened in the meantime to quickly divert attention from issues within the country and forced human beings of all ethnicities, races, creeds, sexual orientations, and political views to unite by helping each other get through it but the horror of hurricane season twenty seventeen had only begun.

Slave Trade East Coast

Before the 16th century, slaves were shipped from East Africa and Madagascar to the Arabian Peninsula and the Indian Ocean. Most of the export of African slaves was in Zanzibar. Zanzibar was where Arab slave traders were abundant. They went deep into the continent or raiding expeditions. Many Africans that were sold into slavery were captured, enemies, people minding their business, or criminals. After capture or sale, slaves were lined up according to size and tied together with heavy wooden yokes about the neck and shackled at the ankles. Some also had manacles that secured their hands behind the back or attached to each other. Shackles were never removed until they reached the coast.

Arabs slave traders enslaved their own along with Europeans, and Africans. They were brutal, preferring female slaves over male slaves. Women were used as instruments of pleasure, yet they were treated as brutally as men as they marched through the continent. Ivory tusks were bought from Africans; they were large and heavy. If a woman was carrying tusks and her child, and became too tired to carry both, the mother was forced to abandon her child or watch as her child was killed to make the ivory easier to carry. Pregnant women were not spared. If they gave birth during the trek and couldn't walk, the woman and her baby were killed.

Not even human decency or consideration of selling the child was given to the woman or to her baby. Some slaves, whether male or female, were hung by Arab slave traders if they couldn't continue walking. It was the price they had to pay for the money traders had paid for them without gaining any benefit. Hyenas, vultures, or any wild animal didn't have to go far to find their next hunt. It took weeks to months for slaves to walk to their destiny of Kilwa or Bagamoyo. If the captured made it to the shores of Kilwa or Bagamoyo, they lost all hope of ever regaining their freedom. It was the last place they would see on the continent of Africa.

Arab traders castrated African male slaves to prevent them from reproducing. Both the testicles and their penis were removed. The procedure was so cruel that only a small percentage of slaves survived the procedure due to excessive bleeding. These castrated men called Eunuchs were used to guard female slaves or concubines.

If a slave survived the weeks to months long foot journey, they were packed into tiny wooden boats called dhows. These boats were no bigger than one hundred and fifteen feet. Two hundred to six hundred human beings were sardined into these boats in whatever position they could fit. Some were stuffed so tightly, that it took days for a slave to be able to straighten their legs after they reached Zanzibar.

WHERE ARE MY CHILDREN?!

Slaves often had no covering from the ocean, heat, or rain. Slaves suffered from thirst, hunger, and seasickness. Others died of exhaustion. If slaves were fed, they were given a small ration of rice and foul-smelling water to chase it down. Sanitation was nonexistent and rapidly spreading disease became a constant companion in all dhows.

Slave traders had to pay duty on any slave that made it to Zanzibar whether healthy or ill. When an ill, infected, or weak slave was discovered, they were chucked overboard. Other slaves died at port before they could make it to market for sale. Slaves were cleaned before they were sold because clean slaves brought in more dirty money. Male slaves, whether men or boys, were oiled and dressed appropriately for sale. Women and girls were dressed and adorned with beaded jewelry, with Henna and Kohl being placed on their eyebrows and foreheads for beautification.

Slaves were always sold in the afternoon. They walked with their owner around the marketplace in the order of shortest, to tallest, and youngest, to oldest. The slave owner screamed out their sale prices as they were paraded around onlookers who were eager to make a good purchase. Each slave was forced to make a mockery of themselves by running or walking to prove their agility. All interested purchasers checked each slaves' mouths, extremities, and eyes. For extra security, traders promised all interested parties that the slaves were free of blemish and disability.

Slaves sold in Zanzibar were needed to work the plantations there. Once an interested party was ready to make a purchase, the slave went to the highest bidder. Slaves who were bought in Zanzibar were treated better than when they made the trek across the continent. Some were given land, time off to take care of their land, and if they were "good," their owners would set them free after a few years of servitude. Other slaves were taken to Oman or other places in the Indian Ocean.

Although this sounds like a happy ending, they were still slaves who never made it back home, and Mother Africa saw it all. She swallowed the blood of her children who died on the continent. She was furious of the blood that was spilled by slaves on their way to Zanzibar, but she knew where those children were. She is not as concerned with those as much as she is concerned with the ones that were taken out of her borders.

Her children were gone, and she wants them back. She heard her children calling her. She has been patiently waiting, and her patience had run out. Like any good mother whose children have not returned to their home, she was preparing to go searching for them. She will never rest until she finds them all.

Slave Trade West Coast

Slaves along the West Coast were sent to the Americas through the middle passage of the Transatlantic Slave Trade. The slave coast consisted of Senegambia, Sierre Leone, Windward Coast, Gold Coast, Bight of Benin, Bight of Biafra, West Central Africa, Angola.

The Transatlantic Slave Trade began in the fourteenth century and lasted well into the nineteenth century. Even after the slave trade was abolished, slavery continued in the new world. Every inch of the slave trade was planned with precision for efficacy and the highest monetary gains. Mother Africa burned with anger because of the evil hearts of greedy men. She has seen the blood of her children

WHERE ARE MY CHILDREN?!

soaked into the soil of every country that took part in its carnage. She has seen her children returned to the dust of foreign lands. She has seen millions of her children walking through the doors of no return.

Most of us have heard of the door of no return located in Ghana West Africa. It doesn't matter if the door was physical or spiritual, every port on the West Coast, East Coast, and Madagascar had a door of no return. Perhaps Africans understood what was about to happen when they reached those doors of despair; perhaps many didn't.

European colonizers in the Americas wanted to make money on goods such as sugar, molasses, coffee, fruit, tobacco, liquor, arms, woven fabrics, salt, ivory, gold, and cotton. African, Arabian, Brazilians, British, Europeans, Portuguese and others sold human beings like cattle into servitude. Africans had a history of being sold into slavery by the Portuguese and Arabs long before the Transatlantic Slave Trade began. In the new world, English colonizers were imported as indentured workers, but there were not enough of them. The indigenous people in the Americas could not handle long working hours of hard labor, and some refused to do it through resistance. After sending the indigenous people to the brink of extinction from disease and conflict, it became more cost effective to pile men, women, and children by the thousands into the belly of wooden beasts. They traveled thousands of miles for weeks to months to become beasts of burden.

Instead of Europeans leaving the children of Mother Africa alone, her children were devalued as being easier and cheaper to use. Melanin allowed Africans to withstand working in the sun all day. They were a hard-working people who were strong and that was what the industry required.

L. A. DAVIS

Even with all the money Europeans slave traders had, greedy slavers wanted to make more. They made so much money off the backs and blood of the children of Mother African that Africans became known as black gold.

Passage to Hell

The Transatlantic Slave Trade was broken down into three passages; Outward, Middle, and Homeward. These passages made up the Triangular Trade. It was called Triangular because the slave trade involved journeys from Europe to Africa, Africa to the Americas, and the from the Americas to Europe which is in the shape of a triangle. Slaves by the hundreds died on their way to ports on the continent; they were the lucky ones. Some were sold multiple times before they made it to their destination. Slaves were never transported by any other means but shackled feet whether they had footwear or not until they entered vessels that showed no mercy.

Each part of this triangle was for money whether it was to sell slaves or to buy and sell goods. Millions of slaves over the centuries of the Transatlantic Slave Trade died on the journey through the middle passage.

The Portuguese were the first to engage in the Transatlantic Slave Trade in the sixteenth century proving it was possible on their maiden voyage. When the Transatlantic Slave Trade began, trips took two to three months from Africa to the Americas. Some took longer if navigators got lost, and some never made it to land once they set sail. With centuries of practice, that trip would go as low as six weeks. Every journey was plotted in harmony with nature. Ships navigated according to the flow of the

WHERE ARE MY CHILDREN?!

Gulf Stream, Trade Winds, and The Westerlies. The Portuguese imported the largest population of African slaves in the Americas than any other country between 1501 and 1866. Though sugar was the primary reason for slavery in Brazil, gold and diamond deposits increased the slave trade.

After the Portuguese proved the journey successful, Europeans, French, British, Spanish, Swedes and the Dutch took part in the deadly sins of lust and greed. Slaves were nothing more than cheap cargo bought to be beasts of burdens to supply cocoa, cotton, tobacco, coffee and to sweeten it, sugar.

Slaves were also sold to work mines for precious metals such as silver and gold. Ironically, slaves were made to cut lumber to build more ships to transport their brothers and sisters whom they would never meet. They produced goods needed for trade working the plantations and household servitude for the rest of their lives. After the abolition of the slave trade in 1807, slaves were still being sold illegally in Cuba and Brazil for a higher price than when it was legal.

During the Outward Passage, European slave ships arrived at the coast of Africa bursting at the seams with goods to trade, barter, and buy slaves. Local leaders were offered gifts and paid taxes for the right to trade. Each region of the slave coast had an item of value they used for trade. Some slaves were traded or sold for Manilla; a form of currency. Some regions traded with cloth, liquor, firearms, beads, and cowrie shells which was a sign of wealth and power.

The slave trade was so lucrative that Barracoons, Forts and other structures were built to house slaves until ships came to pick them up like children waiting at a bus stop.

L. A. DAVIS

Slaves housed in forts at the coast were purchased to be taken on the second, and worst part of The Triangular Trade called the Middle Passage. As Mother Africa travels this part of the slave trade, her fury begins to build. The return or Homeward Passage was the third stage of the Triangular Slave Trade. After slaves arrived at their designated posts, they were sold in slave markets. Trading of slaves provided means for the purchase of sugar, different spices, and other agricultural goods. Slaves could be used as bills of exchange or as a source of currency if money was low. Some ships were cleaned and sanitized then filled with merchandise before setting sail back to Europe for the cycle to begin again. An entire trip through The Triangular Trade could have taken as much as a year.

At no time during The Triangular Trade were those ships of greedy men empty. Mother Africa watched as slavery continued in the United States and slowly became illegal in 1863 with the Emancipation Proclamation which only freed slaves in rebellious states. Two years later, with the drafting and the thirteenth amendment of the constitution in 1865, all slaves were set free; but, were they really?

CHAPTER 2

Rise and Shine

In hurricane season 2017, Mother Africa heard her children calling her while she slept. Although she could hear and feel the agony of her children, she could not see them. When she opened her eyes, she listened to the spirits of her children who had perished on the continent screaming out to her. They pleaded for their family members whom they could hear crying from abroad, but Mother Africa couldn't answer, she didn't know where their family members had gone. The children who had died on the continent and Madagascar during the slave trade so many centuries ago could only tell her that the last time they saw their loved ones, they were heading towards the East or the West. Mother Africa tried to quiet and soothed her children. She listened to their tribulations as they provided lamentations.

To hear her children telling these stories made her heart burned with a consuming fire. Her soul was about to burst with grief as she held back her tears. She assured those lost on her dust that she would go and find their family members, her children, and she would continue to look no matter how long it took her. Mother Africa continued to hear her children outside of her boundaries, but she could not see them. She called out to them, but could they hear her? Yes, they could! They were the ones who had died in the ocean right outside of her borders — the ones who had chosen their own destiny by drowning or who were thrown overboard after the insurrection.

Mother Africa asked her children in the Atlantic Ocean where their brothers and sisters were, but they didn't know. The only thing they knew was the direction they went. Her children told her how much they loved her and chose to die because they could not bear to be away from her. They wanted to know where their loved ones had gone. They could hear them crying and wailing but could not see them. Just like she had promised the spirits of her children who had died on the continent, she also promised her children who had drowned in the ocean that she would go after their brothers and sisters. She told them that she needed their help to guide her as she searches for her children.

Every Cabo Verde Hurricane moves in the direction that her children tell her the slave ships went. She will never run out of places to go because her lost children are so many. As her children in the ocean shared their stories, Mother Africa began to cry. Her rain of tears and grief created a tropical wave cloud.

Mother Africa slowly heated the Atlantic Ocean with her hot tears. The Atlantic Ocean is the cemetery that holds the unmarked graves of millions of her children. She cried over the loss of them so much that on August 27th, 2017, Mother Africa's tropical wave cloud blossomed into a tropical storm. Her hot tears continued to heat the ocean off Cabo Verde until it reached above eighty degrees. When the water reached the best temperature, evaporation occurred and caused her cloud to become bigger. This cloud held her spirit; her spirit of love for her children, her spirit of wrath for those who stole from her, and her spirit of vengeance. As Mother Africa's hot tears created warm moisture, the air moved upwards. As her cloud caused the ocean to churn, she called out to her children. They answered and allowed themselves to be picked from the ocean. As they began to fill her cloud, they began to tell her their stories. The heated air caused by her tears replaced the upward moving air. The air was also heated from the tears of the children she picked up, and from the tears of gratitude of finding them. As Mother Africa embraced her children, their tears caused the cloud to create low pressure.

More of Mother Africa's children were swept up into her cloud causing it to start spinning. As Mother Africa and her children continued to weep, she began to be carried by her winds. She called out softly to more of her children as she loved on the souls of the ones who answered and came to her. She embraced them hugging and kissing them, as they continued to shed tears.

As Mother Africa's cloud carried her children, she asked; "What happened to your brothers and sisters?" "Where are they?" Each of her children told her about the slave traders. The spirit of Mother Africa listened to what her children endured as they walked the continent. "My dear children, if you died on the continent, how did you end up in the ocean?" she asked.

"Our souls went after our family, but we could not find them. Since we couldn't find them, we didn't want to go away from you, so our souls settled into the ocean because that is the last place, we saw them. Some of us were drowned by slave traders because we were rejected at the Barracoons. They couldn't take us back to our homes, so they killed us," her children answered.

"We saw the skeletons of our brothers, sisters, and other family members all across the continent."

Her children told her how they were kidnapped, sold, beaten, starved, diseased, and how their family members were either killed or taken with no idea of where they went. Some of her children within her cloud told her how they were ripped apart by sharks when they were thrown overboard. They told Mother Africa about the horror of having to choose their death, and how they suffered by drowning.

Mother Africa was angry and filled with fury! She asked her children; "Which way did the slave ships go?!" Her children pointed West; she was headed along the route of the Middle Passage. As she traveled the oceans propelled by her winds and her children, she called out to more of her children from the ocean.

Because of her extended slumber, Mother Africa was exceptionally powerful. Every time she called out to her children in the ocean, they answered. Some of her children chose to fight for their survival. Some died on ships that were lost to rebellions, or poor navigation. Some were thrown overboard for sport or money. Any of her children who were folded into the ocean were the ones that answered her. They were so densely packed into her cloud that Irma could not see where she was going.

Hundreds of her children began to form a circle in the middle of the cloud. They lined up next to each other with arms locked to keep them in place. They put their backs against the cloud to open an eye. An eye for their mother to see where she was going and to make a path for their brothers and sisters to enter. The more she howled, the more children were lifted and the more furious she became.

WHERE ARE MY CHILDREN?!

She continued to ask her children, "Where are your brothers and sisters?!" "Where did they go?!" They told her West, so she continued to move in that direction. On August 31st, 2017, Mother Africa became Hurricane Irma.

L. A. DAVIS

CHAPTER 3

IRMA

Irma became a Category 3 Hurricane in one day, and she was just getting started. Here winds were one hundred and eighty-five miles per hour, the strongest hurricane in the open Atlantic in recorded history. Irma's cloud packed with the souls of her children began to grow. She started to decrease in strength due to her eyewall replacement. She felt it was needed since she was so densely packed with her children. She needed a short rest before she hit land. She was going to need all the strength she could gain to find her lost children. Irma continued her voyage, heading towards the Leeward Islands. As Irma traveled, she continued to pick up her children over water. Irma could feel the hate radiating towards her children on slave ships. She could hear and feel them crying for her, crying to feel the freedom of home again. Freedom of speaking in their own tongue, freedom of dancing to the beat of their own drums, and the freedom of being free.

Her children continued to talk to her, telling her of their tribulations. Men, women, children, young, and old spoke to her. In anticipation of finding her lost children, Mother Africa continued to pick up steam becoming more potent with fury. Irma could feel the intense suffering of her children, she could feel their tears, she could hear their cries, she could feel their fear, she could feel them wanting to

35

return to her, and she could hear them calling her from the land, but she couldn't reach them. The pain of her children fueled her rage.

As Irma traveled, she saw how meticulous every part of the triangular trade was planned. Every decision made to catch, purchase, and ship human cargo was done with a specific purpose like an assembly line. Slave traders both men and women figured out how best to secure slaves even if it meant stealing them. Irma watched as frightened Europeans slave traders caught Africans through raids, kidnappings, or through other means. They were too afraid to face the possibility of disease and being overtaken by Africans. To combat this fear, Africans were given the charge to kidnap women, children, and men from deeper within the continent. They didn't dare trespass too far from the coast; no, that was left to the Arabs whose intense lust for money didn't stop them.

Irma knew long before the Transatlantic Slave Trade that slavery was prevalent within her boundaries. Slaves were often sold into household servitude and could be a reason why others had no issues with selling their sisters and brothers in the time of the Transatlantic Slave Trade. Slaves sold on the continent never faced the brutality shown to them like when Arabs took part in the selling of slaves or with slave traders of the Transatlantic Slave Trade.

Some Africans who were captured in battle by other ethnic groups or committed crimes were caught and sold to traders. It was a quick way to make money and to get rid of a community nuisance, but not all Africans took part in the inhumane practice of selling slaves. Some kings refused to sell anyone into slavery whether they were an enemy, criminal or captured in battle.

WHERE ARE MY CHILDREN?!

European slave traders preferred male slaves over female and children, but women and children were easier to catch because men were able to run faster. Slave traders did not care if slaves were skilled or not. They didn't care if they were kings or queens, prince, or princess. To them, they all had the same value of becoming beasts of burden. A skilled slave who could build civilizations in Africa, could build, and create in the new world while other slaves could work the fields. Hundreds of potential slaves died in revolts when they were captured. Irma watched as many were captured without being given a second glance until it was time for them to be inspected. Slaves were handpicked for the one-way trip to the unknown land.

As Irma and her children traveled the ocean, they explained to her how doctors painstakingly inspected slaves while they waited to be shipped from forts.

"Mother, doctors were hired to inspect us to make sure we were healthy enough to make the long voyage," they told her.

"Did they tell you when you were leaving the forts or where you were going?" Irma asked.

"No Mother," they answered. "Only doctors, captains and crew along with the navigator knew when and where everyone was going. No slave ever knew where they would end up because they were too afraid that we would cause an uprising. The best sign we had, was when the doctors inspected us. We knew after that, we would be boarded on ships during the darkness of night," they answered.

This upset Irma as she continued to barrel through the Atlantic Ocean.

"What happened to the people who could not go on the ships?" Irma asked?

"Mother, if the captured were not in fit health, they were expendable. They would be either killed or left to wander homeless, as a vagabond. They were never returned to their home. None of us were allowed to have bad eyesight, rotten teeth or appear in poor health. Men were not allowed to have a slender build with a narrow chest because slave traders were afraid they would get sick even if they were completely fit. If slave ships had to go out quickly but didn't have enough people to fill the ships, slave traders would pay the doctors extra money to allow the slaves to board. They knew they would die before they hit land but all they had to do was count them on their books and file insurance claims against them."

"How would the insurance company know if someone lost a slave?" Irma asked.

"Mother, I don't want to tell you."

"Tell me!" She screeched.

"Mother, they would cut off a body part and show it to the insurance company as proof before throwing them overboard.

"What?!" Irma bellowed; her cloud began to grow bigger and she began to spin faster.

"How long did it take the slave traders to have you board the ships?" Irma asked.

"Mother often many of us were boarded after the doctor checked us all during the night. They did it as quickly as they could because the slave traders were afraid that the crew would get sick or catch a disease. They were afraid we would create mutiny, but we were not allowed to set sail until the ships were full. Many of us died in the middle of the ocean. We could see the land, but we were unable to leave the ship. We chose to fight for our freedom, unfortunately, death was the only way we could get it. We had never been on a ship much less seen the ocean before. The ships would sometimes have rough sea and some of us suffered from seasickness. We were kept in filthy conditions and shackled like dogs." They answered.

"The ocean is so beautiful mother. How can it be used for such evil?" they asked.

"Greed takes every beautiful thing and makes it ugly my children," Irma answered.

Irma listened as her children continued to talk to her, explaining the things they had experienced.

"Mother, even though the slave traders had heavy firearms against us, they were terrified of us. We feared them also. We had never seen people with guns and such fair skin before. They told us they were going to take us from here to eat us while they traveled the ocean. We would get together and fight! but they were too strong against us."

The children in the cloud continued to cry hot tears of rain. "Stop crying children," Irma said calmly. "They told you they would eat you?" Irma asked.

"Yes mother," they did.

"These men were Europeans, Spaniards, British, and other fair-skinned individuals. They told you those ridiculous stories to frighten you! They were not going to eat you! They were going to sell you! I am going to bear down on them with such fury that this will never happen again!" Irma exclaimed.

Irma thundered as her children continued to talk to her while she traveled.

"Many of us onboard the ships killed a few crew members, but we saw many crew members killed before they got on the ships. Some of us spilled the blood of those men at the shore. We watched as their blood fell on the rocks. Ten percent of slave ships had uprisings. We are Senegambians and we refused to be taken without a standoff! Along our coastline, we had the highest number of uprisings and they always brought in extra firepower here! In 1725, we chased crew members from the ship!"

The Senegambian children within Irma's cloud burst out with such cheering that there was the sound of thunder clapping out of the cloud. It was the first time Irma felt such pride come from her children since her journey started.

While Irma and her children continued to travel, they saw something horrifying. They watched as thousands of her children decided to jump overboard before ships set sail. It made Irma's soul grieve. Some of her children in the cloud started crying harder than before. They watched as their brothers and sisters were treated like cattle. Slave traders had until the next morning to return slaves they decided were unfit for the journey. If they did not return the slaves by the following day, like a used car without a warranty, all sales were final.

Mother Africa saw slave ships ranging in size from small merchant vessels to large vessels at her coastline. Some ship owners wanted more deck space and room for sleeping quarters. Some ships had no sleeping quarters and crew members had to stay on deck no matter the weather. Some slave traders preferred smaller ships because they required a smaller crew with a faster turnaround. This decreased the chances of captain, crew, and slaves from being plagued with illness.

Loose packing meant slaves had a better chance of survival. As Irma continued to travel, she continued to pick up her children from the ocean. No matter how tragic their death, they were filled with love and joy of being reunited with their mother. All the children within the cloud welcomed them. The first ones they met were the ones holding the hurricane eye open. They could not embrace them, but their smiles shone with love. They knew they were finally home.

The children in Irma's cloud continued to tell her of their stories as they watched some slave traders using tight packing to transport slaves. The more slaves transported at one time brought in more monetary gains even if some died along the way. Irma saw one ship packed so tightly that there was no room for her children to move.

"Mother, I was in the belly of one of those ships. I had to lay on my back, and I suffocated on my own vomit. We were always shackled together on our backs and I became sick with the movement of the waves. One day, the person next to me became enraged because I had vomited on him when I turned my head. I eventually became so weak from vomiting that I could no longer turn my head. I died that morning and my body was sent to the ocean and my soul went with it." Some of the other children opened their mouths in horror. Another child in the cloud told his story.

"Mother," On our ship we were packed like spoons. The entire trip the only thing I saw was a naked ass while someone else saw my dirty feet. What do you think happened while my face was down there? the only time I was free from that sight was when we could go on deck for fresh air."

The children inside Irma's cloud laughed so loud that it sounded like thunder.

"Quiet down Children," Irma scolded them. There is nothing funny about this.

The children quieted down as the continued to tell the story.

"Many of us had accidents on each other. When we were not shackled to the boards, fights would break out. Some of us couldn't understand each other and that made it worse. While I was being transported, I contracted tetanus through an open wound while in the tween decks. The doctor on board did not have anything to treat me. I died shortly after because the filthy conditions did not help. I was thrown overboard and there is where my soul rested."

No one in the cloud spoke for a few minutes. Irma must have been thinking because the next time she spoke it was like a sound never heard before.

"Where did your brothers and sisters go from that ship?!" Irma screamed.

The children answered her, "Mother keep going on this path; we will tell you when to turn."

While traveling, Irma and her children saw how low the decks were built inside those ships. They were made to prevent her children from revolting by removing their ability to stand. They saw how slaves had their wrists, elbows and ankles rubbed raw to the bone from the constant movement of the ocean against unpadded planks and shackles that bound them. Irma and her children became horrified after witnessing a ship who packed her children sitting between each other's legs. Long rods secured their shackled hands to the ship with such low space that they could not move or lay down. They sat in that position day and night as they tried their best to get comfortable sleep. Some of the children in Irma's cloud started crying with their hands over their eyes.

WHERE ARE MY CHILDREN?!

"Mother, some of us were forced to sit in that position. We could not use the relief buckets because we had people sitting between our legs while long rods secured us to the ship. We were forced to sit in each other's waste. When our backs hurt, we would lean back on the person behind us."

Irma and her children could see every story told on this journey. They cried with grief which fueled Irma's anger. As Irma's rage intensified so did her strength. Traders did not consider the unsanitary issues tight packing would force slaves to endure. To many, it didn't matter. The only thing that mattered was getting as many slaves to port in as good enough shape to sell and trade for merchandise.

Mother Africa's children, both men, and women were often covered in urine, feces, blood, vomit, or sores. It was either their own or someone else's. Buckets used to hold excrement were left inside the same decks with her children. There was no way to escape the suffocating stench. These deplorable conditions bred disease which spread amongst the slaves. They were so hot and filthy that crew members dared not go down into the tween decks unless necessary. These natural, filthy, and unsanitary saunas that used no electricity or hot stones sent able-bodied men and women to their graves during the night while they slept.

Irma and her children were forced to watch in agony as some of her children decided to choose their own fate. They shared their stories of hopelessness; hopelessness that forced some to choose death. Others were forced to decide to live, and others were never given the choice to decide. Irma's children continued to talk to her.

"Mother, I was in such despair that despite having netting placed around the side of the ships, I found a way to jump into the ocean. All of us on the ship had seen crew members decide to jump and we were happy about it. I felt that I lived for nine months in water, that dying that way was right. I had no idea how painful a death it would be. All these centuries in the ocean, I had never found peace. This is my first time finding my peace. I am sorry for feeling happy about the crew members that died. At least you came for us, those who are not of you had no one. They were as sad as we were, or they wouldn't have jumped. Please forgive me, mother."

"There is no need to ask for forgiveness, child. There are thousands of you in this cloud that jumped, and I am here to take you all home." Irma replied.

As Irma traveled the ocean thousands of her children continued to fuel her. The choice of her children jumping overboard was their form of defiance due to the inhumane conditions and abuse by crew members. Irma watched as shackles and manacles were strategically used to bind her children together by twos or threes onboard to prevent movement as much as possible. Her children continued to talk.

"Mother, we were forced to wear manacles and shackles all the time. The women didn't have to wear them after they came onboard but we had too. Shackles and manacles were painful, and they caused cuts and sores to our skin. I saw some slaves cut all the way to the bone and it caused them to become infected."

"I'm listening!" Irma replied.

"Slave traders were scared we would cause an uprising; they were right. We were always planning in our heads what we could do to get off these floating things. If we couldn't move comfortably, then we couldn't commit suicide or cause an uprising. There were men who went crazy because they would go to sleep and wake up next to a dead person who was shackled to them. The only way they could get the dead person off was if we could come on the deck and the slave traders would see it. If we were shut indoors, they would have to wait. Sometimes when the storms came the body would start to rot in the heat of the tween decks."

Irma and her children listened and saw what their sisters and brothers were saying. It frightened them. The children were unsure if Irma could get any angrier but soon, they found out the answer.

"Mother!" "Yes children," she answered.

"We could walk around the decks with the children. Slave traders didn't want anything to do with them, but it brought in money. If we took care of them, they were free to run about. When we first came on board, the slave traders branded us under our breasts while the men were branded on their arms. We felt like animals because we had never had a hot iron placed on our skin before. We never complained because we felt so badly for our brothers. Even though we had a hot dirty place, at least we didn't have to remain shackled."

Irma continued to call out to her children, and they continued to enter her cloud. Some of the children said, "Mother look! These were the best days of our voyage. Good weather was our best friend because it allowed us to go on deck for fresh air, sunshine, food, cleaning of the ships and dancing."

Irma watched as slave traders used dancing as a form of exercise for her children and entertainment for the crew.

"We loved dancing, but our brothers didn't. They were forced to dance to the songs of improvised drums and whips." This infuriated Irma. Some of the male children in

Irma's cloud became furiously angry as they watched their brothers and sisters improvising instruments of music with whatever they could find.

"Children; why are you angry?" Irma asked.

"How could they like dancing?! Some of us were thrown overboard for not dancing! Some of us couldn't understand what they were telling us to do! Some of us refused because it was too painful! Some of us refused to dance because the captain and crew would start laughing at us and it caused us great shame! Some of us were shackled next to uncoordinated men, and the shackles cut into our skin until it started bleeding! You women and the children remained unshackled; it was easier for you to dance!"

"Brothers please forgive us!" the women cried.

"To these evil people dancing was something for them to make fun of, but we danced to the spirits of the ancestors and our beloved Mother Africa. Dancing gave us the strength and the will to live. It strengthened our souls. Music was communication to whomever we worshipped."

"Sisters! The sting of those terrible whips tried to take our strength away, and many of our brothers died because of it!" the men in the cloud yelled.

Irma intervened. "Quiet children!" she scolded for a second time.

"This is not a time to start arguing! I need you to pay attention!"

"My sons," Irma said calmly. I am watching as your sisters danced for those of you who couldn't. They saw how torturous dancing was for you because you remained shackled. They knew that the crew members didn't care if you wore shackles and manacles that tore into your flesh, or if the chains rapped against your ankles. Your sisters knew that the crew or captain didn't care if you were shackled together by two or three and couldn't dance in unison. They knew that crew members strolled the deck beating those who refused to dance, and they danced harder to spare you!"

Irma and her children watched as men had their backs stripped by long whips or another nasty shortened whip called the cat-o'-nine-tails. This whip was shortened to the cat or handle of the strap which had nine strands of cloth, coated with tar, and tied in a knot at the ends causing massive damage to their skin. Irma began to scream with fury at this point! She continued to barrel toward the West, to find her children she had seen in those terrible conditions on those ships and the ones who were calling her. As she traveled, the sounds of her children that called her were getting stronger.

"What is this, that I am watching!?" Irma raged.

"Mother, we were fed twice a day; once in the morning and once in the evening if we were lucky. We were only given a pint of water to drink each day. When we were fed, it was not enough to keep us full. We were so thirsty we begged for rain. We were fed according to the regions that we entered the ships. Not from the regions most of us came from. Some of us were fed cornmeal, boiled rice, or millet. Others were fed yams that were stewed, while others were fed cassava, cassava flour, or banana-like fruits. If our owners were feeling particularly generous, they would give us just enough meat to keep us healthy."

Irma began to pick up speed with her fury! "You stole my children from a land where there were farmers! They raised their own crops, and the villagers came together to make sure that no one went hungry and this is what you reduce them too?! My children were hunters and gatherers who respected the land! They brought back fresh meat and shared what they had! They used their skins for clothing and shoes!"

Irma churned the ocean with a massive force. The more she saw, the angrier and stronger she became! The children in her cloud continued to tell their stories.

"Mother, there were times when we were not allowed to come above deck when the weather was bad. When we weren't allowed to go on deck, the crew would give us raw tube vegetables such as sweet potatoes. Some slave traders threw the raw vegetables to us, knowing there was never enough, and great fights would ensue due to hunger. Our brothers were shackled and didn't get fed because no one wanted to go down there."

Irma and her children listened as they heard millions of hungry bellies lamenting with growls.

"We were so hungry that some of us looked for crumbs of spoiled food below deck and in the holds. Fights broke out when the slightest morsel of food was found. We drank from stagnant pools of water left by leaky ships that were mixed with remnants of the unsanitary conditions of illness, feces and every manner of bodily fluid."

Irma howled louder, some of her children in the cloud put their hands over their ears.

"My children were taken from a land that flowed with streams and rivers where water was so clean that even the animals shared its coolness, and this is what you do to them?!"

Irma continued to barrel. More children began to join their sisters and brothers within the eyewall to keep Irma's eye open. She was becoming stronger. The more she heard and saw, the more furious she became. Though the children should have been at peace, some of them became frightened. They could feel Irma getting stronger and faster. Her children weren't sure if they should continue to tell her stories, but Irma spoke up! "Children!" she yelled.

"Yes mother," they answered.

"Keep speaking to me, I need to know what happened to my children and where they went, Irma replied.

Her children continue to tell her their stories. "Sometimes we were fed our second meal of the day in the late evenings. We were given beans most of the time. Beans were cheap, plentiful and protein dense. They were boiled until they were very soft and then drenched in a greasy palm oil, flour, and water mixture. To hide the unappetizing taste of this devil's brew, the crew covered the beans in a vile spicy pepper topping. Many of us could barely stand to eat it. Some were so hungry they would eat it and then throw it up as soon as it hit their stomachs. We would find it comical, but the crew didn't."

Irma watched in fury as crew members and the ship owners were fed the choicest of food.

"Mother!" some of the children called.

"Yes children!" Irma responded.

"Some of us were not as fortunate as those ships. We only got fed the left-over scraps if there was any, and only if the crew wanted to share. Some of them would purposely throw the left-over scraps overboard while we watched. When food sources were low, we were not fed at all."

Hundreds of her children in her cloud started crying.

"Mother, we were thrown overboard with others to make sure that there was enough food for my sisters and brothers. We were weak and tired, and they refused to feed us. Before they threw us overboard, they told us that all they had to do was file an insurance claim once they got to the port and no one would know the wiser. To prove to the insurance company that they had purchased us, they cut off our ears before throwing us overboard!"

While Irma burned with fury, the other children listening to this story began crying tears of rain as others continued to share their stories.

"Some of us were warriors who chose to go on food strikes as a form of rebellion. Crew members tried to discourage us from becoming involved in this rebellion by forcing our mouths open with manmade instruments of torture. Some of us were threatened by putting hot coals to our lips if we didn't eat. We refused to make others rich by selling us."

Irma continued to call out to her children in the ocean. As she called them; her children continue to talk to her about their experiences.

"We enjoyed the beautiful weather while we cleaned the filthy hulls and decks of our ship. In most cases, ships were never cleaned. Many of us died on these beasts of disease and pestilence. When the sun went down, we had to return to their death trap in the tween decks. The tween decks were dark and suffocating because air couldn't circulate. The sick and dead were housed amongst the living. Feces and urine flooded the tween decks."

Irma watched as all her descendants on slave ships were treated inhumanely, but she knew if the men were treated badly, the women were treated worse.

"Mother we were unshackled but we were not allowed to come out of the holds. They were filthy and hot as an oven. The crew members, captain, sailors, and navigators put us closer to the deck because we were easily accessible to them.

WHERE ARE MY CHILDREN?!

They used us as bedwarmers. We were handpicked and taken to living quarters of the captain and crew to have sex."

The women in the cloud started crying.

"Stop crying children, you are safe here," Irma interrupted.

"Mother, some of us were beaten and raped for refusing. After I was raped, I felt defiled. When I went back to the hold, the women beat me; some even spit on me. The hold was already a terrible place. A woman had a nail pounded into her head while she was asleep because the men came and got her in the night. She didn't even have enough time to scream because no one heard her. The next morning no one would admit to it and everyone was beaten until the perpetrator told on herself. She begged for her life, but she was thrown overboard without a thought, and we saw her being eaten alive by sharks. I jumped into the ocean to cover my shame. I didn't care if the sharks attacked me. It would have been better than what I had to deal with internally and inside that hold."

Many of the women inside the cloud started to wail because they experienced the same story. One lady had been raped so badly that she died from her injuries. Another woman spoke up.

"Mother, they never returned us in the darkness. They would wait until the morning light. The men would bring us back when everyone was on deck. It was done on purpose to cause us shame. Many of us had never been with a man and none would touch us after that. Many of us could not understand each other, but we would do our best to protect each other. When the men came to get us out of the hold, we would fight them. They would threaten to shoot us. Some of us didn't care. We were going to save ourselves and our sisters. When the men managed to get us out of the hold, and we came back, some women who tried to save us turned on us like rabid dogs. I don't know if they were jealous that we were picked or if they thought we were worthless because we had been defiled. Please forgive me! All I know is that I am here, and I am finally at peace. None of us who fell into that ocean was at peace. Our deaths were too terrible for that. Thank you for picking me up. I can now go back home and rest."

Irma and the other children within the cloud embraced and loved on the souls of these women.

"I promise you, my children. I will avenge your death!" Irma said savagely.

Irma continued to increase her wind speed, sound, and strength. Of the precious human cargo, it appeared that the little children were lucky. Irma watched as small children would run the decks of the ships unshackled. She watched her warriors take advantage of this opportunity by using the children to communicate amongst other slaves to plot mutinies. Irma realized that the slave owner didn't understand that they had taken men and women of strength who could think and plot. Because they could not understand the language, slave traders saw no value in the engineers, hunters, gathers, strategists, and kings who had built civilizations. Mother Africa knew that some of her children had unbreakable spirits, and no matter the size of the ship, they would rebel at any opportunity.

Irma and her children watched as some crew members were beaten by ship owners for mistreating and striking the slaves. If slaves were brought to market with skin that was not smooth and clean, they would be too hard to sell. Natural maladies were persistent, and there was no need to

WHERE ARE MY CHILDREN?!

add other issues with slaves getting infections due to their opened skin. Crew members and slaves were often lost due to dysentery, yellow fever, malaria, flu, scurvy, smallpox, dehydration, measles, and mental health issues such as depression and claustrophobia.

Irma became enraged! She yelled, but it sounded like winds to the human ears.

"My children have never seen such pestilence! What is this? You have broken down their natural immunity by malnourishment! I will destroy every place where you greedy slave traders planted your feet!"

Some slave ships got lost during the Middle Passage due to poor navigation. Food sources would run low, and hunger would set in. Being stuck in the middle of the ocean on ships where crew and captain had no idea of where they were going, caused depression to slaves and crew members. Irma watched as these illnesses also were inflicted on her children. Some were driven crazy due to claustrophobia. Some of her children developed a mental illness because they were taken from their homes and sold without the knowledge of where their family members were if they would ever see them again, or where they were going. Her children were no longer free to live their lives off the land. They would no longer be able to see man, animals, and nature work in perfect harmony. Irma saw how her children were isolated. They were unable to communicate because slaves were often sold with slaves from other regions that did not speak the same language.

"Mother!" some of her children called.

"Yes, dear," she answered.

53

"Were we purposely sold with other brothers and sisters who didn't speak the same language to cause isolation and to stop uprisings?" they asked.

"No, you weren't," Irma answered.

"Your brothers and sisters were brought from different areas of the continent to the boundaries of the coast. Ships had to be filled as quickly as possible. In other areas where forts were built to house your brothers and sisters, they were set to sail once the doctors said they could go, and the ships were full. It didn't matter where they came from so long as they were able-bodied. Ships also stopped along different ports of the slave coast to pick up your brothers and sisters. Greedy slave traders wouldn't have taken the time to make sure slaves did not speak the same language, served the same master or whomever they worshipped. Money was too important to worry about such things. Do you understand?" Irma asked.

"Yes, Mother," her children answered.

"Mother, some of us saw our brothers and sisters lose their mind. They were beaten with whips and clubbed to death before being thrown overboard. Irma watched as her children lost their minds. As she listened, she continued to pick up her children from the ocean while she broiled with anger.

"Welcome my beautiful children. Come and find refuge and protection!" Irma said.

"Thank you for picking me up. I and several others had an eye disease. It spread through the tween decks like fire because we were so tightly packed together. Some who got the disease were left blind. We were not beaten for having the disease because the crew was too afraid to touch us, but they showed us no mercy either. We were quickly thrown overboard to prevent our disease from spreading."

The children in Irma cried as they listened to their stories.

"Drowning was a terrible death. I was able to see my brothers and sisters drowning as I was forced to tread water. I watched many of them struggling in the water. They were fighting to catch their last breath. I was the last one still in the ocean as I watched the ship leave us behind. I became tired and made peace with what was about to happen, and then I drowned."

During this trip, many children who jumped or were thrown overboard were reunited with their families. Some had chosen to jump overboard together. Irma's children hugged as they continued their journey to help Irma to find her children.

"Which way did your brothers and sisters go from here children?!" Irma asked.

WHERE ARE MY CHILDREN?!

The children answered, "Go, Northwest, Mother."

While traveling closer to warmer waters, Irma and the children in her cloud saw gams of sharks. They saw how the gams strategically followed each ship like they knew something was going to happen. They watched as crew members threw the sick, and dead overboard. It didn't matter if it were male, female, child, or adult. It didn't matter if it were crew members or the captain. The only person assured their lives would be well taken care of where the navigators, but some did succumb to the deplorable conditions on slave ships like many of the others.

Some of the children in Irma's cloud covered their faced and wailed.

"What is it, children?" Irma asked.

"We were forced to stand at the sides of the ships and watch as gams of sharks used their razor-sharp teeth to tear into flesh and crunch on bones. In some cases, gams were so immense that the slapping of their fins killed slaves and crew before they could drown. Each shark tried to be first to dine on the taste of human flesh. Within seconds they would be gone with not even a shred of clothing being left. We had not seen this before, and we screamed in terror as we saw people being ripped to shreds. Some of the crew members looked on with dread but said nothing. Other crew members, captain, and navigators laughed at us."

The children in Irma's eye were so traumatized that some of them lost their focus. They almost closed Irma's eye.

"Get back in place!" Irma screamed.

Some children in the cloud were those that had been torn apart by gams of sharks. They closed their eyes and screamed.

WHERE ARE MY CHILDREN?!

"Mother, no! Please, we do not want to see this. Please go faster from this place so that we do not have to witness our deaths!

Irma sped up in strength and rage as more of her children packed against the eyewall to keep it open. Irma knew that her dead children were nothing more than inventory lost, and no inventory brought no pay. Her children knew this also, and they used their knowledge of war or the human instinct of fight or flight to cause uprisings. Some of her children benefited from being warriors or in military service. If they weren't trained for war, they learned while on these terrible journeys. Knowledge of war gave them an advantage. Speaking in a language that only her children knew gave them more of an advantage as they could plot without being found out. If they had no common spoken knowledge, they learned to communicate from the will to live.

"Children!" Irma called.

"Yes mother, they replied.

"Please continue to tell me your stories. I am almost close to land mass."

"Yes mother," they replied.

"In one uprising, we successfully overtook a slave ship and killed almost every crew member."

The Children inside Irma's cloud started clapping and cheering. To the human ear, this would have been thunder and lightning with the howling of high winds. Her children continued to find ways to resist.

"Mother, we used anything we could find to cause maximum damage. We used shackles and manacles." Some of her children said.

Irma knew that one of the most dangerous things in this world is a person without hope. When there is no hope, there is no fear and fearless people will do what they need to do to survive. Irma and her children watched as ships were lost in uprisings due to fire or explosions on board. They watched a ship sink after an uprising in 1785. All of Irma's children lost in that uprising was picked up by her cloud. Irma and her children watched as crew members used heavy firepower against them. They were agonizingly punished once the ships were brought to order. Some of her children were thrown overboard to drown or for sharks to feast. The children inside the cloud started screaming!

"Mother look, there! There were other ships watching as our brothers and sisters were being punished so that others would not do the same."

"I see it, children!" Irma replied.

"Those traders thought it would stop them from declaring their freedom, but it didn't. I will pick them up from the sea, and I am going to find the rest of my children. Hold on; we are close to land mass; I can feel it!"

Irma continued her journey as she watched the ocean. She shook with fury as she watched so many of her children meet their ancestors from those ships. Five men to every three women were sold into slavery. Only three out of five slaves made it to their destination due to the deplorable, inhumane, and unsanitary conditions on those ships.

After weeks to months of sea travel, slave ships would make it to their destination, but they were not allowed to dock. Ships were unsanitary. They were floating boxes of evil and disease, and they stunk. Slaver traders would drop anchor a few miles offshore, and slaves were rowed to port in smaller boats which had been stored aboard the ship.

WHERE ARE MY CHILDREN?!

Irma saw her children practically starved on the long journey. It was a deception of health that slave traders perpetrated on those eager to make a purchase. To make sure slaves brought in the largest amount of money available, they were fed so that they would look healthier for auction before ships arrived at their destinations. Irma watched as slave traders who had her children with scars, sores, or skin that was worn to the bone, filled with hot tar. They screamed out in pain as the hot sticky liquid touched their opened wounds. She saw how slave traders took palm oil and mixed it with ash then massaged it into their skins so that it would appear smooth and healthy. Irma could no longer control her fury!

For a second time, Irma and her children watched as they faced the trauma of separation as everyone was sold. What infuriated Irma more than anything was the fact that her children were sold to make others rich, yet there was no respect for them. For centuries Mother Africa saw through her hurricanes how her children were removed from her perimeters, and how her children and their descendant were treated, and how they are still being treated today. She has seen the people who mistreated them, and she kept score. She made a promise to go searching for her children to bring them home. She goes out searching for them and has cursed every destination and those who participated in the act of greed.

As Irma got closer to land mass, she could hear her children calling out to her, and she could feel the souls of her children. She asked her children in the cloud to concentrate and guide her in the direction she should move. She did not want to hear any more stories because she was so furious at this point that becoming any stronger would cause more devastation that even she predicted.

Irma could hear the prayers of wailing women and intercessors from all cultures. The prayers, tears, and outcry were much clearer now. It was coming from multiple places. She could feel the pain of her children's fear, loneliness, and uncertainty. The closer she got to land, the stronger it felt and the angrier she got. Irma asked her children, "Which direction did your brothers and sisters go?"

The children never argued about which way to go. They all sang in unison, "They went Northwest, Mother!"

On September 6th, 2017, Irma's wrath fell on Barbuda, Anguilla, St. Kitts, Nevis, St. Martin/Sint Maarten, the British Virgin Islands, the United States Virgin Islands and Puerto Rico. Time and order of destruction varied. The Caribbean chain of islands are many. Some islands are close together, and some are farther apart. This did not matter to Irma who had grown so big that several islands felt her wrath at the same time. Her eye which was still being held back by her children did not hit every island directly but for those that felt it, knew that she had not come to play.

CHAPTER 4

Irma's Path of Destruction

Barbuda

Approximately 2:00 a.m. on September 6th, 2017, the menacing Category 5 hurricane Irma and her children made landfall on the island of Barbuda. Her tentacles of wind reached St. Barth, St. Martin/Sint Maarten, and Anguilla. Irma waited until darkness fell to crash into Barbuda with a vengeance. Disasters that happen during the darkness are far more frightening than when they happen in the daytime, and Irma wanted everyone in her path to be frightened.

Irma had grown into a three hundred and seventy-eight-miles vast juggernaut. Her winds were one hundred and eighty-five miles per hour, and Barbuda laid in the center of Irma's eye. The first things this Category 5 monster destroyed were boats and the shoreline. Cabo Verde Hurricanes have an extreme dislike for boats, seashores, and ports. These are the places that the children of Mother Africa were deposited, and to them, all boats are slave ships. Irma was no different, and she toppled boats in hopes of finding her children. Irma hit land, howling loudly, "Where are my children!?" she yelled.

Her voice was made of thunder and lightning! She drove through Barbuda like a freight train destroying whatever she could with fury. She howled through the winds.

"You've stolen from me, and I am coming to steal from you! Where are my children?!"

No one was able to answer. Many occupants of Barbuda went over to their sister island of Antigua. Irma had threatened the island, and many decided to leave. For those who chose to ride out the tempest, they couldn't answer because they couldn't understand what Irma wanted. Even if they knew, occupants were too frightened to speak. Prayer was the only language they spoke at that time.

People hid to save their lives. These islands held the bones of descendants, of a people who had lost their original tongue. Irma called for her children in every language that represented the countries they were stolen from. No one could understand her.

"Children!" She screamed.

"Yes, mother!" they answered.

"Do you see your brothers and sister?!" she asked?

"No mother! we hear and feel them, but we cannot see them. Their descendants are the only ones we can see, and they are running for shelter. They are extremely frightened mother, please have mercy on them."

"I am showing them mercy!" She answered.

"I will show mercy to all of these islands because my children's descendants are my descendants. For some reason, you cannot see what I see as you did over the ocean!" If the souls of Irma's children answered while she was over the island, Irma couldn't hear them because her fury was so much. She asked her children whom she picked up from the ocean if they were sure their brother and sister were here?

WHERE ARE MY CHILDREN?!

"Yes Mother, but their blood has been spilled into the soil, and their bones returned to the earth, they cannot answer you!" they replied.

Irma could feel the agony of her children, her grandchildren, her great-grandchildren, and their descendants. She cried hot tears of rage as she scrubbed the island turning over homes destroying electrical poles and businesses. Everything not battened down was turned into torpedoes. Rooftops were ripped from man-made structures. Irma and her children watched as her children and their descendants were bred like livestock on an island which was used as a nursery to raise children who would later be sent to Antigua to work the plantations. Irma became more incensed! She screamed, but it sounded like thunder to the people.

"You used my children to plant your crops for export?! You sent them to neighboring islands and North America to do the same! I am going to strip these islands bare to avenge the back-breaking work of my children which was used to make others rich! Where are my Children!? Give them to me or I will make history this very day on this island!"

Irma uprooted trees and turned over cars with her winds of rage.

"Britain you emancipated everyone except Barbuda! Why did my children have to find their own freedom?! Why did you lock them in pens like animals when you caught them?! Didn't they have the right as a human to be free?! Even the ones you claimed to have set free had to struggle to survive by working the plantations for a widow's mite. That is not freedom!" Oh, did this make Irma angry!

L. A. DAVIS

Irma scrubbed Barbuda for thirty-seven hours. She was still scrubbing the island while beating the other islands in the Caribbean chain. No other storm in history has ever stayed over land that long. She left ninety-five percent of the island destroyed. She moved her focus from Barbuda to Anguilla without moving. Her children told her that more of their brother and sisters had gone to the other islands.

Anguilla

On September 6th, at 8:00 a.m while still beating Barbuda, Irma set its sight on Anguilla with her Category 5 winds of fury. She churned slowly as she continued to pick up her children from the ocean. Even though her eye was over the ocean, her tentacles of one hundred and eighty-five miles per hour winds beat Anguilla and the other islands with a fury. She churned up the seashore and threw boats in every direction without care. She passed over a building of worship that was built in 1830 on the backs of her children. Irma was furious.

She howled, "I can smell the perspiration of my children! You used their sweat to mix the mortar as you would use water while they broiled in the noonday sun! You took the word of God who created me and twisted them! You took his words and reconstructed them to enslave my children!" Rage continued in Irma.

"When you dropped my children in these wretched places, you omitted Gods words from your Bible to keep my children enslaved! What is this slave Bible that you created and used against them!? Where did you hide it!? You removed any word that showed my children's strength that sustained them; the strength that sustained their

66

ancestors who were stuffed into the guts of those filthy, sea creatures! You then had the arrogance to take my builders of temples and civilizations, my engineers, and architects and forced them to build this place of iniquity!

You taught my children who were great warriors to pray to a God whom you created to enslave them and to keep my children in mental bondage! You told my children to bow their heads in humility to the God that created them, but in truth, they were bowing their heads in humility to you because you thought you were God!" Irma wasn't finished with her wrath.

"Where are my children?! I can hear them calling out to me all the way from home! What did you do with them?! Where are they?!" Irma screeched.

"Children!" Irma called.

"Yes Mother," her children answered.

"Are you able to see your brothers and sisters?!" She asked.

"No mother! but we are sure the ships dropped them here. We can hear them calling to you, they are ready to come home to you, but they cannot because they are within the soil from where they came, and it is final!"

"Irma became even angrier!" final?! It will never be final until every soul of my children is returned to me!"

"Why can't you see your brothers and sisters as you did on the ocean?" Irma asked her children.

"We are not sure mother!" They answered.

Irma watched as her children were beaten to give up their spiritual beliefs and adopt those of their captors. Some hid their practice. Irma had no objection to any of her children worshipping who they wanted to, but she became enraged as she watched her children being beaten because of it.

"You ignorant foreigners! You forced my children to give up their spirituality and adapt to your ways of worship because you were cowards! You were afraid of them! What were you afraid of?! While my children had their heads bowed, their eyes closed and their backs turned, you stole everything from them! You were so greedy that you didn't see fit to leave them alone! You not only stole their dignity! You stole their souls! You stole my children from me! You robbed me! The God that created you, the God that created them, is the same God that created me and this land in which you have pillaged! God had nothing to do with building this place, your evil did! I can smell the blood, sweat, and taste the salty tears of my children in the seams of this wicked place! Just as you destroyed and reconstructed the word of God who created me, so shall I destroy your evil works!"

Irma destroyed that place of worship. When Irma was finished with Anguilla later that day, she left with ninety percent of the island to include the infrastructure destroyed.

St. Kitts

Hurricane Irma hit St. Kitts, and her sister island of Nevis at 8:00 a.m. on September 6th at the same time it was beating Barbuda and Aquilla. Irma's winds screamed as she hit the shoreline of St. Kitts destroying every boat in her path.

Irma watched as the French and British settlers colonized the island. Irma screamed for her children. "Where are my children?!" Again, no one could understand her. Irma did not care. She was too angry. Irma watched as her children were killed in wars between the

WHERE ARE MY CHILDREN?!

British and French colonizers over land that did not belong to them.

"You stole my children!" Irma belched, to the French.

"Mother!" her children interrupted.

"Please do not interrupt me children until I am finished speaking! I know this is frightening for everyone including you, but this must be done. I heard my children in agony all over these lands and I am going to do what I can to find them!"

"Forgive us, mother," they replied sheepishly.

"Go ahead children, what is it?" Irma asked.

"We are starting to see what you are seeing but most of the trouble is on the sister island. We see little children there."

"Little children?!" Irma repeated.

"Yes, mother, they are maimed and in the fields!"

Irma showed St. Kitts mercy. The island sustained only ten percent damage. Irma damaged some of St. Kitts infrastructure, housing, and infrastructure.

Nevis

While hurricane Irma was battering St. Kitts and Anguilla, she continued to pick up more of her children from the sea as she battered the sister island of Nevis.

"Can you see your sisters and brothers?!" Irma asked her children.

"Yes mother, we can hear our brother and sisters and they are crying! We can feel their anger and sorrow. We can see their descendants and they are frightened." The children answered.

"I see them too!" Irma replied.

Irma and her children watched as their brothers and sisters worked the plantation fields to produce Sugar cane, Indigo, Ginger root, and Tobacco, for greedy slave traders and consumers in Europe.

They heard their cries from the tip of the whips. Their skin had been bloodied from beatings, darkened by the noon sun, and drenched in sweat. They watched their loved ones cut tall, thick stalks of sugar cane. To quench their thirst and stave off starvation, slaves were chewing on the husks and hiding the remnants in the dirt so no one could see. They watched as slaves had gotten caught and were beaten mercilessly.

Irma and her children roared over the island with fury, destroying whatever she could find. The children within her eye held on to each other tighter and watched as her children were bitten by insects like fire ants, centipedes, and mosquitos who found favor in the sweet juices of the sugar cane and in the people, who had to cut them.

They worked from sunlight to sunset as her children used their knowledge of cultivating, planting, and harvesting sugar cane. Her children were so well versed in horticulture that sugar cane took over tobacco and all other forms of agriculture of export because it made greedy slave owners rich.

Irma became volatile when she saw her children dying from starvation. She cried out in her winds.

"How can lands so lush in vegetation and fruits allow my children to see starvation?!" She thundered.

"Mother look over there!" her children yelled.

Irma and her children watched as little children hobbled around the plantation after being stricken with yaws. They had no shoes on their sore filled feet that had calloused over leaving them deformed.

Irma roared furiously!

"My grandchildren were working these fields with their pained joints and sores on their feet and bodies?!"

All the souls that Irma picked up from the Atlantic Ocean since leaving Cabo Verde closed their eyes, put their hands over their face and wailed. Her children who had their backs against the eyewall continued to lock their arms, but they closed their eyes and wailed as tears streamed down their faces. Watching children being bred in Barbuda was bad but seeing little children working the fields with yaws made Irma abominable.

"Where are my children?!" she screamed as torrents of rain, thunder and lightning came from her.

No matter how much she howled and screamed, no souls of her children from the islands would answer. They couldn't for they were in the soil. The same land that her children had to till after burying their descendants.

Irma howled, "Great Britain! Where are my children?! You will pay for your desecration on these lands! This land brought you wealth on the backs of my grandchildren! These were babies! Why didn't you tend to their diseased bodies?!"

Those in Irma's eye held fast and continued to keep her eye open as she barreled through the island. Irma was so angry about slave owners using her grandchildren to plant that she destroyed much of the island's agriculture, livestock, and infrastructure.

"Children! She asked.

"Yes mother!" they answered.

71

Were your brothers and sisters dropped on this path or should I go back into the ocean?" she asked.

Her children replied, "Mother stay on this path; we can feel them here!"

Irma stayed on her path of destruction and approached the island of St. Martin/Sint Maarten.

St. Martin /Sint Maarten

Hurricane Irma hit the dual French and Dutch island of St. Martin and Sint Maarten on September 6th, at 8:00 a.m. Irma continued to howl, "Where are my children?!" Irma understood that when her children were taken from her land, it was all motivated by greed, yet she could not help being astounded as to the treatment her children had received.

Irma had much of her natural resources pillaged from her body for centuries. She saw it being done in Brazil and on this island. Irma and her children watched as greedy slave traders robbed the Americas of their natural resources. They watched as colonizers argued over human beings whom they felt they owned and how they made them scrape the land of its precious resources.

Irma caused homes on the islands to break before blowing them apart as Irma's wrath continued.

"The indigenous people of these islands never fought over their natural resources! They respected what came from the earth including each other! When you came to this land you found the people here and you abused them and raped the natural salt resources of this island until there was none left! You didn't have enough respect to leave any behind because you were greedy!"

WHERE ARE MY CHILDREN?!

Irma howled with her ferocious winds.

"You brought my children to this land! "Where are they?! Give them back to me so that I can take them home! For two hundred and twenty years you held my children in bondage on this land! You were so wicked that you didn't set my descendants free at the same time! Why didn't the Dutch release my descendants until fifteen years after the French!? You abused my children and dared to call yourself the friendly island?!"

Irma and her children watched as their brothers and their descendants worked the tobacco fields. Irma howled for her children as she saw how they were beaten while they picked coffee beans and cotton that left their hands bloodied and gnarled. This, another island was flowing with plantations of sugar cane. Irma and her children were reminded of little children working the field with their diseased bodies in Nevis, and she was on a destination of pure destruction.

Irma called out for more of her children. As her children continued to be picked up through her well-defined eye, they hugged and kissed her and found space within her gigantic cloud of unforgiveness. Irma continued to destroy boats, hoping that her children would be on these vessels of doom, but they were not there. They were all empty, and this made her filled with more fury.

"They were fleeing mother!" her children yelled.

Irma sat still for a minute and watched as thousands of the islanders had evacuated St. Martin and Sint Maarten to Guadeloupe before she got there. Airframes were sent in to remove people that wanted to get out in hopes of escaping her wrath.

73

Those who had no recourse but to wait out this great tempest were terrified of Irma's nature. Occupants in their homes felt and heard her fury. They were scared, and they cried out to God for mercy. Some of her children who were just picked up from the ocean found a comfortable refuge within the cloud said, "Mother, let's go this way, perhaps we will find our brothers and sisters there! Our other brothers and sisters cannot answer you because they are in the soil; maybe the other islands will allow us to find them!"

Irma demolished St. Martin/Sint Maarten. She decimated the airport to stop others from fleeing.

Saint Barthélemy (St. Barts)

Hurricane Irma became angrier by the minute as she continued her path of destruction.

"Which way did those ships take your brothers and sisters children?!" Irma asked.

"Mother they went that way!" As they pointed toward St. Barts. Irma's eye went over St. Barts on September 6th around noon.

Irma continued to pummel the islands with her fury destroying everything she could before she got on land and before she left. Her children within her cloud assured her that their brothers and sisters had been deposited on St. Barts. Irma and her children watched as the Swedish in the 1700s sold her children to slave traders on St. Barts and returned to Ghana for more.

"I curse you this day with influenza! Your fleet will be stricken so that you will think twice before returning to this land! Where are my children?!" she howled. "Where did you take them?!" "Give them back to me!"

WHERE ARE MY CHILDREN?!

Irma and her children watched as her able-bodied older children were taken from her land. They were not allowed to return to their final resting place that held the bones of their ancestors. Irma and her children watched as her daughters were sold to men to be used as whores.

"You took my daughters and forced them into submission! You took them from behind like dogs because you could not bear to face them like men! You bulged their bellies with your seed for profit!"

Irma demolished St. Barthélemy by destroying the tiny island's infrastructure. She destroyed its hotels, homes, all forms of communication, electricity, and means of travel.

"I am finished with this place!" Irma' screamed to her children.

As Irma continued to travel, she pummeled and grated each island to a punishing degree. She left inhabitants of the Caribbean chain in fear. Some occupants had to hold doors closed during the entire time she was overhead to prevent them from being sucked out of their homes to their deaths. She was on her way to American and she caused unimaginable damage as she came to reclaim her children.

United States Virgin Islands
(St. Thomas, St. John, and water island)

Irma continued to steamroll through the Caribbean. She was not concerned about being tired. Her children continued to hold her eye open, and she had become bigger from picking up so many of her children. Hurricane Irma hit the USVI, on September 6th, at 2:00 p.m. She was especially angry because of the history of her children on these islands consisting of St. Thomas, St. Croix, St. John, and Water Island. Irma and her children hit three of these islands with devastating results.

Irma hit St. John with her eye only twenty-five miles away from the tiny jewel. Irma and her children watched as the first slave ship hit the shore of St. Thomas In 1673. They watched as many more hit the shorelines after.

"What have we here?!" Irma asked.

"Why do these tiny islands have so many plantations on them?" She asked quietly.

The children inside of Irma watched quietly as Irma spoke with thunder. Irma and her children watched as her children were picked like fruit off the island of St. Thomas by slave owners and taken to other islands to work.

Irma exploded! As she watched St. Thomas St. John and the islands surrounding it.

"These islands have fallen under several flags and the people have been abused by all of them! My children were brought here and abused! They belong to the large land from where I hear my children crying and moaning the loudest!" Irma and her children watched in anger as the islands surrounding St. Thomas was used for breeding livestock which slaves had to take care of. That was not her objection. You used my children who were skilled goat herders to raise and care for your livestock! They told you how to feed them so they could produce more and make your money belts fat! You allowed my children to go hungry even with your bounties!" Irma bellowed.

Irma and her children saw a trend within these islands with their lush vegetation, clear waters, and sunshine. Even in these places of such natural means of food and beauty, there was hunger, despair, and ugliness amongst her children.

WHERE ARE MY CHILDREN?!

It made Irma angry! "You stole my children from a land of plenty! where they could hunt and eat as they pleased! no one saw starvation because neighbors could not put rags on their cuts while their neighbors bled from their own. My children did not know poverty! They were kings and queens; prince and princes and you bring them to another land of plenty where all they saw was hunger! You left them in poverty! And, you mistreated them! That wasn't enough for you! You went to her neighboring island of St. John and conquered that island and abused my children there!"

Irma screamed into the abyss of her winds. "You stole my children to come to this place where you mistreated them and had the nerve to fear for your lives because they outnumbered you! These Emeralds of the Sea have been passed from one flag to the other and sold to the highest bidder for cheap to people who had no interest for the people but only for themselves! You never saw the true value of the people or for their land! You sold them for a penny to the place that I am now going to search for my missing children! The cries of my children are very strong in this place and I will take this land and shake it upside down until you give my children back to me!"

As Irma and her children kept moving, she continued to look for her children on the islands of St. Thomas, Water Island, Hassel island, and St. John.

Irma screamed into the islands "Where are my children?!"

"Mother look over there!" her children cried.

Irma and her children watched as slave ships stopped at the shores because the indigenous people and settlers refused to work the land. There were always resistance and the indigenous people paid the ultimate price. Even if they were able to sustain themselves with homemade weaponry, they were unable to save themselves from disease they had never seen or heard of before.

The stories were the same across every island of the Caribbean. Her children were hoarded like cattle on ships and sailed across an unforgiving ocean in unforgiving conditions. Irma and her children watched as slaves were auctioned off like animals to greedy Danish investors who owned sugar plantations.

"Ah! That dreaded sugar cane! That is what those plantations were for," Irma sighed.

Irma and her children watched as her children also cultivated and harvested cotton and indigo for owners whose only concern was money.

The children inside of Irma screamed as they lifted more of her children out of the ocean!

"Why did you scream like that Children?!" Irma asked.

"Mother, the feeling of the people here is so heavy. They are so very frightened mother. Please show them mercy! They have endured enough. We see what they have endured but our brothers and sisters will not answer because they are in the soil. These people are different from all the other islands and we are not sure how or why. Your wrath seems to be intensified here. Please, may we go?!"

"I will move on shortly, I am beginning to get full, but I am not finished here!" Irma replied.

Irma returned her attention to St. John, she screamed out loudly howling in her winds.

"Where are my children?! You diabolical slave traders left my children to suffer through droughts! When my children fought for their freedom, they overcame you! You had the nerve to send in troops from neighboring islands to come back and kill them! You then placed them in bondage again! You publicly humiliated them by whipping them like they had no feelings! You removed their limbs! Limbs that did not belong to you! Limbs that the God who created me gave them! You had no right! You chose to hang them from trees to try to show your superiority! Trees that you forced them to plant! Why didn't you set them free?! For this discretion, I will scrub this entire island clean of its vegetation! I will show you who has the power by forcing you to wait until nature decides to give everything back to you!"

Irma devasted the islands of St. John, St. Thomas, and its surrounding islands. St. Johnians were left with no means of getting off or on the island as the ferrying service was destroyed. All methods of communication were gone. The only way to get in or out of the island was by small boats. Irma destroyed buildings and left beautiful pristine beaches eroded with no sand to beautify the shoreline. Irma destroyed schools, hospitals, and homes.

The sick had to be taken to Puerto Rico and the mainland for care. Some perished after losing their will to live. Others were lost for months because proper records were not kept to show where they were sent. Some died from the trauma of having to leave the islands to go to a foreign land just like many Africans died when they had to leave their home to go to a foreign land. Irma left tourists who came for vacation, and students who came from abroad to study at the local university stranded. Some had never experienced a hurricane and wanted to get out but couldn't.

After Irma passed, heroic young men from the neighboring islands of St. Croix and Puerto Rico got into boats to bring food and supplies against official warnings of the arrest of anyone who tried to go against rules set in place for safety reason. Irma looked on these individuals with a smile.

The British Virgin Islands

Irma and her children powered into the sister islands of the USVI (Tortola, Virgin Gorda, Jost Van Dyke, Anegada and Necker island) on September 6th, at 2:00 p.m. Though islands were close together some were more fortunate than others. The British Virgin Islands were not. Irma and her children looked over the islands and saw the hardship that slaves on the island of Tortola had to endure.

"Where are my children?!" Irma cried.

They watched quizzingly at the island because there were few slaves on the island as compared to many others. Irma didn't move for a minute. She watched as slaves were given their own plots of land to toil.

Over the years in the 1700s, Irma could see that land was no longer readily available and her children began to starve. Irma kept seeing these lush islands that her children tilled being kept from feeding them. Irma burned with fury! She saw how more populated the island became, the harsher her children were being treated.

Irma screamed as flashes of lightning lit her up!

"You whipped my children until their backs were left with holes like a road filled with potholes! You separated my children in their houses; I never saw this before! What is a house slave? What is a field slave? How did you decide that?! These were brothers and sisters on the same ship, and you put one in charge of each other! You allowed them to be whipped by their brother?! You had to have known this would cause division!

WHERE ARE MY CHILDREN?!

Irma's voice became like a freight train.

"How dare you Europeans pit my children against each other by having my children fall beneath the lashes of whips by their brothers?!"

Who told you that my children are beneath you?!" Irma barked.

"It was okay for you to strike my children, but if they struck back, you punished them severely! You murdered my children when they remembered who they were, and they defended themselves! Well, I am here to bring justice!"

Irma turned the BVI from a beautiful green to a dustbowl of brown within twenty-four hours. The best way to describe it was to compare it to a bomb that had dropped and exploded upon impact.

Puerto Rico

On September 6th, 8:00 p.m., Irma plowed into Puerto Rico. She continued to call for her children as she headed to the United States mainland.

Irma and her children watched as a free African man touched the shoreline in 1509. He came with Spanish conquerors and invaded the island killing the native inhabitants through labor and disease.

"What is this?!" Irma howled! How can an African who is a free man in this rare occurrence kills innocent people without question? How can he be a part of this carnage?! His skin is not of a fair but of a dark complexion."

The children in Irma's eye began to wail again as they watched their sisters and brothers branded.

"Mother, we cannot watch this! This was worse than when we were branded!" They cried. Irma's Rage went rampant.

"To make sure that my children would not regain their freedom, you took hot coals to their foreheads?! I can hear them screaming!" I can hear the sound and smell the stench of sizzling flesh?!"

As the hot coals touch their brother and sister's forehead and they screamed, the children inside the cloud began to scream at the horror they were watching.

Irma was enraged! "You impregnated, the indigenous people and my children to remove their African roots! You asked my children who were made free on my land to come to this land to support your fortress after you emptied the mines of its resources! You forced them to lose their tongue and adapt to your own! You forced them to remove their spirituality and forced them to worship your God! You freed my children on paper, but you did not do so in spirit! You were so greedy that you hired more of my children to produce your sugar! You promised them freedom if they fought for you, but you didn't do it until years later and you have treated them as outsiders ever since! You stole their language, music, and arts then you stole their heritage!"

"Mother!" her children cried.

"Yes, children!" she answered.

"Do you remember when we said that those islands sold under multiple flags felt different from all of the other islands?"

"Yes children," Irma answered.

"We feel the same way about this land, but we are not sure why." Her children replied.

WHERE ARE MY CHILDREN?!

"Children, I am not sure either, but I am growing full and weary and still have a few more stops to make. Irma, skirted the island of Puerto Rico leaving areas flooded and without electricity."

On September 7th, 2017 Irma continued to pick up her children as they told her the direction her brothers and sisters went. That day Irma hit The Dominican Republic, Haiti, and the Turks and Caicos.

Dominican Republic

On September 7th, around four in the morning. Irma continued her carnage as she continued to call for her children. "Where are my children?!

Why don't you answer me?!"

The children inside of Irma continued to tell her, "Mother, we can hear them calling for you, but you will never find them because their bones are mixed in with the soil It is no use mother!"

"Then if their bones are mixed with the soil, then the soil is what I will take!"

Irma headed towards the island of Hispaniola which is broken down into the two countries of Haiti and the Dominican Republic. Irma passed to the North side of the Dominican Republic. She and the children inside of her cloud watched.

"Children look; can you see where these children came from?" Irma asked.

"Yes, Mother they came from West Africa where they were known to be great warriors like many of our family members, but they did not come straight from your land

Mother, they came from Spain! Why did they come to this land?" the children in Irma asked.

Irma replied, "They came here for the same reasons the others did; it was greed! Over the years they purchased and brought more of your sisters and brothers here to work these plantations after they killed off all the indigenous people through hard work in the gold mines, and famine. The indigenous people were killed off in masses by the thousands for no other reason than for them being here! Your brothers and sisters who were educated people were reduced to working as maids and farmworkers!"

Irma began to pummel the Dominican Republic. Irma and her children saw something as insidious as the children who were forced to work the cane fields. They watched a scene that was more recent. It was far away from the centuries that her children went missing and it made her and the children within her angrier!

"Do I see children working as domestic help?!" Irma asked.

"Yes, you do Mother!" the children within her answered.

Irma belched out her fury as her winds whipped anything loose into the air crashing into buildings.

"You wicked inhabitants of this land! You take my descendants and turn them into prostitutes?! You make them clean your homes and pick your goods?! You did this by crossing your borders into the land of your neighbor! These are little children! The descendants of your own land before you had borders! How dare you?! You enslaved these children and worked them like mules! Then you demanded money for their ransom when they ran away to their freedom! You take the descendants of architects and

WHERE ARE MY CHILDREN?!

force them to build your places? Well, this very day I will destroy them!"

Irma wasn't finished.

"You deported your inhabitants across your boundaries because their skin was darker than yours! You did not care if they didn't speak the tongue or had no family there! Did you feel you were better than them because your skin is lighter?! You are not! You are of them! You were once one people! You murdered over twenty thousand of your neighbors who lived on this land! Why did you do such a wicked thing?!

You hate your neighbors, yet you hire their children to clean the beds that you sleep in, the dishes that you eat from and the lands that grow your crops! Some crossed your borders because they could not afford to take care of themselves! You did to them what the Spaniards did to your ancestors who were my children! You are my descendants, and you cast shame on this land! Some of these children have absolutely nothing yet you take the very little that they have left, their hope and their dignity!"

Wrath was churning as Irma ranted.

"They risked their lives to come to this land for peace of mind, and this is what you do to them?! You work them in the hot sun for hours each day without enough clothing to shield the sun from their skin! You whip their bodies if they did not work fast enough for you! You barely fed them even when they swing cutting instruments in your cane fields! Why did children have to suffer in these fields?! I have seen this before for centuries, and today I promise, it will be no more! I will come back and touch you so harshly that you will think that what was done to you before was a blessing!"

"What will you do to them mother?" We are frightened!

"I have you, there is no reason to be frightened, but they will have much to be frightened of before I am done here," Irma said calmly.

Irma turned her wrath back on the island.

"These are not yet men or women; these are children! Little boys and girls! Do you think if they had a choice, they would cross the border at the risk of death if they could escape elsewhere?! Or, is that why you treat them so harshly?! You are wicked people, and I will punish you for this! I will ravage you so that you will never forget this day!"

Irma devastated the Dominican Republic causing massive damage with flooding. Powerlines were down, with a much-needed bridge that bonded Haiti and the Dominican Republic destroyed. Over twenty-four thousand people had to be evacuated with hundreds of homes destroyed.

Haiti

While Irma was battering the Dominican Republic, she also battered Haiti.

"Children, did your brothers and sisters go this way!?" Irma asked.

"Yes, Mother; many are on this land that is split by boundaries. Keep on this path, and you might find them. As we get closer to that large land mass the cries are getting stronger!" her children answered.

As Irma continued to look for her children, she continued to shed a deluge of tears causing massive flooding. She couldn't find her children. She continued to hear their souls calling her, but she couldn't locate them. She could only see what they had endured. Her heart was full of rage and despair as she continued to travel the route her children in her cloud told her to go.

Irma and her children watched the island of Haiti as she and her children saw the one named Christopher who came ashore with the intentions of pillaging, rape, and murder! She shook Haiti as she watched the people welcomed this traveler and then saw him kill the innocent. Irma became enraged!

"You were a stranger to this place where the people welcomed you! You murdered the indigenous people on the landmass of Hispaniola. You defiled the bodies of my daughters and you forced them into hard labor after bringing war and disease! You returned to your native land and left your comrades behind to do your evil bidding! Why didn't you take them with you?! Why did you leave them behind?!"

Irma and her children howled as they watched the indigenous people give their lives in the gold and copper mines.

Irma was furious.

"You wicked people! You took the kindness of strangers and used it against them! How could you be so cruel?! When these people were seeking their freedom, you brought in domesticated beasts to find and kill them for everyone to see! To starve them to death with your wickedness, you burned the fields that you yourselves depended on for your wealth! How evil! You tried to wipe them from the earth, and when there were not enough of them left to bring in your wealth, you came to my boundaries to steal more of my children! well, I am here to find them! Where are my children?! Give them back to me!"

Irma and her children watched with venomous anger as the son of the one name Christopher was encouraged by a priest to enslave Africans and take them to the new world.

"You are a priest; a supposed man of God from the Catholic church! You encouraged the enslavement of my children to be sent to the new world! The son of the one named Christopher commissioned the slave trade to this island!"

Irma boiled with a vengeance!

"You men of the cloth who call yourselves holy! The representation of God you call yourselves! How dare you steal my children from me?! How dare you take my children under the guise of God! Through your greed, you imprisoned and defiled my children by bringing them to this place! To this day you have left your influence on this island! I will bring shame on your church! Your secret truths shall be exposed to the world!" Irma screeched.

The French went to the western side of the land mass in hopes of cultivating indigo. They changed their money crop to sugarcane like many of the islands after they disrespected the soil and it refused to continue to be fruitful.

Irma and her children watched as the Spanish and French went into battle over land that did not belong to them.

Irma said, "Look at what arrogance does to people children!"

"What do you mean mother?" her children asked.

Irma answered, "Arrogance cause people to fight over what belongs to others because they think they are entitled to it! They think they are better than us, and they steal from the righteous!"

WHERE ARE MY CHILDREN?!

Irma and her children watched as little spots started to be erected.

"What are those, Mother?" the children asked.

"Those are sugar mills children; I do not like sugar cane fields, and I do not like sugar mills!" Irma replied.

The French built mills so quickly that it made France rich off the backs of my children. Sugar production has put millions of my children into bondage and into the earth, and Mother Africa made sure that over the centuries she dried them up! The French also cultivated coffee in these lands which made your brother and sisters plentiful in this land. They fought back, absconded into the mountains, and resisted their captures."

Irma paused briefly. "They had been forbidden to practices their religious beliefs. Beliefs that made them feel more connected to me."

"But, Mother look! They are killing themselves and their children!" they cried.

"Yes, children, they wanted to find their way back to me, but the soil took them. Close your eyes, do not look until I tell you too. Continue to hold my eye open so that I can see. We have a little room left for more of your brothers and sisters, be still as I call them to me."

As Irma continued to move, she called more of her children from the ocean who settled into her cloud of peace. "Open your eyes children," said Irma.

"Look at how your brothers and sisters who are your descendants prepare to free themselves! Watch as they kill their captures and burn the cane fields with a terrible fire!"

Haiti sustained heavy rains, and a much-needed bridge between the two countries of Haiti and the Dominican Republic was washed out. Heavy rains caused flooding, destroyed roads, and knocked down power lines. Two souls were lost on Haiti when a tree fell into their home.

"Children, show me which way the ships took your brothers and sisters?!"

"Mother keep going North," they answered.

"Yes, Children! I will find as many of my children as I can hold before I stop!" Irma answered.

Later that day, her eye moved between the island and Turks and Caicos at one hundred and seventy-five miles per hour.

Turks and Caicos

September 7th, at 8:00 p.m. with a vengeance, Irma and her children barreled into Turks and Caicos with her one hundred and seventy-five miles per hour winds as a Category 5 Hurricane. These islands were not as fortunate as Hispaniola. Irma continued to pick up children from the ocean in hopes that they could tell her where the last place was that they had seen their brothers and sisters. They watched as slaves were sent to Bermuda to collect salt after the British occupied it. Freed slaves who had fought against American with the British were thrown out for treason.

Many of Irma's children were Creole born into slavery. With a desire for freedom in a country who saw no value or worth in them, they decided to do what they needed to do to gain their freedom. They cultivated and harvested cotton.

Irma and her children watched as her children were brought from her shores to work salt mines. The children in the cloud started laughing when one of their brothers talked about traveling with a buttock in his face during his trip until he died. For the first time, Irma and her children were laughing as weevils, and other tempests destroyed the cotton industry on the island. The laughter to the human ear sounded like rain pounding on galvanize roofing. They weren't laughing for long.

Irma noticed something here that she had not noticed since her children boarded the slave ships weeks before. She noticed that slave owners required the same number of men, women, and children to work these salt ponds. Irma remembered that in the sugar cane fields there were seven men to one woman and whatever number of children she had. Although Irma was angered over her adult children being taken into bondage, she became diabolical whenever she saw little children working in the fields. Irma and her children watched as men did the hard work of raking salt while children and women bagged and carried salt for waiting ships who needed the nutrient to cure their foods that slaves would never enjoy!

"You men of evil! Irma shrieked!

"You allowed my children to bake in the wind and sun for your delicacies! You did not preserve the family for their good but yours! You calculated that if the family structure stayed together that they would self-populate to make your cellars fat and to reduce your need to purchase more of my children! You went to my shores and stole! Well, I have come to retrieve them, and you will give them back to me! You refused to allow them their freedom unless they were born free! How long did they have to wait for that? Three hundred years?! For three hundred years you worked my children in those watery holes until they went blind from the sun beating on the waters, sand, and salt!"

"Mother, will we ever see all of them? These men are so evil!"

"I am not sure children, maybe one day you will," she answered.

Irma's fury rose.

"You didn't take care of my children even as their health failed! You allowed them to live in unhabitable lodging! I will stir up the salt of the sea and dump it on your shores so you will never in your history use my children to mine your salt fields again."

Irma left the Turks and Caicos in darkness. She snapped poles like toothpicks causing power loss to Grand Turk. Because the electricity was out, water was unable to be produced. Irma left flooded streets and major damage to the infrastructure of the island.

Bahamas

Irma was beginning to lose strength; she was moving closer to the large land mass that she heard most of her children crying from and she was full of her children. Irma hit the shoreline of the Bahamas on September 8th, 2017. She raced in at five in the morning as a Category 4 storm riding on one hundred and fifty-five miles to one hundred and sixty miles per hour winds. Although devastated, the Bahamas escaped the full fury of Irma.

"Do you see your brothers and sisters, children?!" Irma asked.

"No, Mother but we can still hear them calling you! This is terrible!" they replied.

Irma and her children saw ships by the thousands ride the waves of the Atlantic Ocean lining the shoreline of the island. They had come from the island of Bermuda,

England, and America after fighting on behalf of the British in the Revolutionary War.

"Mother, why are our ancestors leaving the mainland for this island?" The children asked.

"They are trying to find freedom just like you are my children, do not judge them!" Irma said sharply.

"Yes, Mother," they replied.

"The Royal Navy freed some of my children while on the ocean, but they had no way to get back home to me. Their bones are ashes now; they never found peace!"

Irma became angrier!

"You wicked Americans! When laws were enacted to free my children, you refused! You are so greedy that the people had to pay you with blood money to allow my children to be freed! I will pummel you with my sledgehammer of fury! Where are my children?!"

"Mother! Listen, our brothers and sisters are screaming from the ocean for you! We have never heard our brothers and sisters calling to you like this before!"

Irma was so angry that she pulled her children and the ocean from the seabed. Irma wanted to frighten those who could see that she meant business! She left the ocean floor devoid of water for two days! Irma left destruction throughout the Bahamas, toppling cars like toys. There were downed power lines, uprooted trees, and roof damage but no substantial infrastructure damage.

Cuba

Irma and her children moved West, towards Cuba on September 8th, with Irma's southern eyewall slamming into the North side of the island at 8:00 p.m.

93

L. A. DAVIS

Irma was the first Category 5 Hurricane to hit Cuba since 1924. She was beginning to become dismayed and weary. She was full of her children from the ocean but none from the land. Her wind speed decreased to a Category 3 Hurricane with one hundred and fifty-five miles per hour winds. Her children within her eyewall continued to keep her eye open.

Irma and her children watched as ships came to the Cuban shoreline with over a million of her children within their seams. Just like the other islands, Irma watched as her children used cutting instruments to harvest sugar cane overtaking Haiti as the biggest cultivator of sugar for greedy investors abroad.

Though Irma was tired, she still had some punch left in her.

"You greedy beings that are not of me! You stole my children, and when the pressure came on your shoulders to stop, you brought in the Chinese who were treated just a little better! You Spaniards have raped these islands with your debauchery and pillaging! To make yourself look and feel better in the eyes of the world, you allowed my children the right to food and clothing! You decreased their toil and their punishment as if you were doing them a favor!

But when laws were enacted to keep families together, you broke them up! You broke them up because of your selfish pride! You are hypocrites! If my children broke your rules, you beat them like animals, but you would not abide by the rules set by your authority! You felt you had the right to beat my children into submission because you were afraid of their power! Well, you will learn this very day that I am the authority and I have the power! I will not have mercy on you!"

WHERE ARE MY CHILDREN?!

Irma wasn't finished and continued her rant.

"You rebelled against the law because you wanted my children to live by your work hours. You put them in huts and locked them inside like criminals with no concern that if a fire came, they couldn't escape to safety! You kept your minds in the prison of fear that allowed you to do this! You fill your huts so tight, that my children could not find a peaceful place to rest! You put them in the belly of these dwellings just as you put them in stagnant, unsanitary walls of the ships! Even the sun goes to sleep for eight hours you wretched beings! I see why my predecessors dried up your wells of sugar! I will dry up your pockets and scatter you as the wind scatters ashes from this place!"

Irma blew her winds of fury forcefully!

"You underestimated my children! I infused my female children with my spirit of a warrior! More than anything, they wanted their freedom, and you forced them to defile their bodies to gain it! You bred my daughters like sheep so that my descendants could work your land! You selected them by weeding out the weak from the strong! You gave my children conjugal visits like a prisoner for the sole purpose of impregnating my daughters because you killed so many of my children under your whips!

You sold my grandchildren to the highest bigger and forced their mothers to the fields if you did not find her children to be of prime quality!"

"Where are my children that you stripped of their dignities?!"

"You hid them away in confinement for as long as you pleased! They are no longer there! Where have you taken them?! Irma squalled! You sent my children crazy in their solitude! You did not feed them; you starved them in this place of plenty! You let them sleep in their own waste! Even my children whom you forced to reproduce were not spared!"

Irma did something strange, she slowed down to seven miles per hour, and she went back to a Category 4 Hurricane.

"Mother, why have you slowed down? Do you see our brothers and sisters?!"

"No children, I am watching something far more terrible, and I am growing weary. I need to preserve my energy. Do not look at this sight children! All of you close your eyes right now! I will tell you when to open them!"

"Yes, Mother," they answered.

Irma watched as slave owners dug holes, but she didn't know why. There were thousands of them. She continued to watch. What she saw, would shake her to her very being!

Irma watched as some of her male children were shot on the spot and killed after some struggle, but she could not see why. As she continued to watch, she began to grow in strength with rage!

"You dirty female whoremongers! You forced my male children to defile your bodies knowing that death would come on swift wings if they were caught! You calculated when you were free to do so without the knowledge of your husbands! My children did not belong to you! Nor did you belong to them! My children were of great strength and stature! You could not keep your mind off their physiques or their endowment, and you could not contain your sexual curiosities and desires! You threatened my children with death by threatening to tell your husbands that they forcibly defiled you if they refused; You liars! When you became impregnated, you did not take the blame! You told your husbands that you were forcibly defiled! The babies were either killed or sold!"

The children in Irma's cloud became increasingly Frightened! Thunder, torrential rain, winds, and lightning was flowing out of Irma's cloud.

Mother, what is it? can we look now?" her children asked.

"No, Children, I am not finished! don't look until I tell you too, or I will send you back to the ocean! No one should ever see this, and I am not finished with these evil doers!"

Irma concentrated on her destruction.

"You ate off the monies that these babies brought into your homes as they were sold, and you had my children killed instead of telling the truth!"

The children within Irma started screaming as Irma howls became deafening.

"There is no reason to fear children; keep your eyes shut!" Irma yelled.

"Yes, Mother!" they cried.

Irma could not believe what she was watching! She watched as thousands of her male children were strapped and beaten with whips! These weren't weak men; they were strong men who could snap a neck with their hands in seconds.

"Why are they not fighting?!" she asked silently.

Irma watched as slave masters who had desires for men, sexually defiled her male children! Her sons were emasculated in front of the entire slave colony to include their family members! large crowds were called to see this strange show of force. After the men were whipped, they were strapped to the ground or strapped to bows, bent over, and defiled from behind! Irma watched as Men were forced to watch as other men sexually defiled their women through rape in front of their entire families! men and women were also forced to perform sexually in front of everyone! This was to make sure that the land was populated without having to import slaves. Irma was weeping. She was pouring down her tears of rain on the land and the ocean. She could not believe what she was seeing.

"They sexually defiled my children! I will pour out my tears of rain on this land to cleanse it! Where are my children?! Why are none of them on these lands answering me?! Why were none of the people who had endured such shame been able to come to me!?" Irma asked as she poured out torrents of rain.

"Mother," some of her children cried!

"Yes children, do not open your eyes yet!" she warned.

"Our brothers and sisters on the land did not dare to take their lives or their families would have had to pay the price!" the children told Irma.

"They had to endure their broken spirits until their last breath. We too were sexually defiled on slave ships. We are the women who jumped into the ocean. We jumped because our shame was too great! We jumped because we had become impregnated and could not deal with such shame! We were taken to the rooms of those men on those ships, and when we were put back into the holds, we were shamed and beaten by the other women because we were considered dirty! Death was better because we knew we would get back to you!"

When she saw these pictures, Irma became angrier than she was before! The last scene before she left the land made her angrier than anything else she had seen on her long journey! Irma was so angry that her cloud began to turn blue from lightning strikes!

"Those thousands of holes I see! You dug openings in the earth and made my daughters lay down to hide their seed! Some seed they carried was of your making! You flogged them until their blood seeped into the earth not giving reprieve to their screams! To ease your guilt, you tried to heal their wounds with salt which made them writhe in agony! You beat my daughters in their swollen bellies until they spilled the seed on the ground! Seeds that were planted in the earth because you killed them!"

Irma poured fury on Cuba as they had never seen! She was so angry that she began to wobble! Weather forecasters were unsure exactly which path Irma would take. Irma lashed the island of Cuba for twenty-four hours, as she sat over the island watching her children be abused. Her path could have ranged from the Gulf of Mexico which had just been battered by Hurricane Harvey.

"Children, you may open up your eyes now! I am ready to go! Where did your sisters and brothers go from here?!" Irma screamed through her winds.

"There are calling from a place called Florida mother," they replied.

Irma destroyed shorelines of every island. Some wholly destroyed to the point that they may never return to their original glory.

These were the places her children first hit land; their footprints still left in the sands as they walked to their new destiny. Irma destroyed agriculture in every island that her children planted and infrastructure that her children built. She dried up export in many of the islands for the abuse caused to her children. Irma began moving, making a sharp northeasterly turn towards Florida. Once she went over open water, Irma strengthened again to a stronger Category 4 Hurricane, but she was growing wearer with each hour. She called out to Mother Africa for help and she sent Jose who was coming to her aid.

Florida, Georgia, North Carolina, South Carolina

Irma's last stop before going to sleep was the Southeast portion of the American coast. On September 10th, Irma hit Florida and weakened to a Category 3 Hurricane with winds of one hundred and fifteen miles per hour, but she soon increased her winds to one hundred and forty-two miles per hour. She had a few things left to say before she took her children to their final resting place. Back home to her land, where they could finally rest.

Irma's wind bands spread as far as four hundred miles from her center. Irma and her children watched as her children were brought to Florida while under Spanish rule. Even after the emancipation proclamation, slavery did not end. This burned Irma with fury! She screamed over Florida.

"Where are my children?! You kept my children in bondage even when other states had set theirs free! You waited until one of the worst parts of history to release my children while you were ruled under the Confederacy! I curse you Florida! I will ransack your coast this day! I will release my fingers from my clouds to tear your domiciles apart and scatter them like you did my children! You will forever be my target! Your name does not represent who it says you are!"

WHERE ARE MY CHILDREN?!

Irma released tornados on Florida as she carried the souls of thousands of her children. She could not find her children on any land mass of the Americas and she was tired. Irma scanned the land as her remnants moved into the state of Georgia during the afternoon hours.

Her children within her cloud screamed and covered their heads.

"Why did you release your hand's children?! Why are you covering your heads?"

"Look, mother! Look at what they did to our brothers and sisters!"

Irma had weakened, but she mustered enough strength to give one last voice of rebuke! Irma and her children watched as slave owners sheared the thick black wooly hair from the heads of her children and were horrified to see it being stuffed into their fine furniture and pillows.

Her children holding her eye open finally released their locked arms as they held their heads as well.

"Children! There is no need to cover your heads; they cannot touch you! You are safe! I am getting ready to take you home to your eternal resting place!"

Irma continued to screech as she whipped her winds screaming.

WHERE ARE MY CHILDREN?!

"You wicked people! What kind of human being would think of such a thing!? You have stolen so much from my children that you even stole the very hair from their heads to bring you creature comforts that my children were not allowed to experience! My children were given hair of a different texture and strength what was greased with natural oils and braided into elaborate styles to show their uniqueness! They learned to hide food within their braids because you starved them so! My children were kings, queens, princes, and princesses! I gave them these crowns to remind them of their greatness! You stole their crowns from their heads! You forced them to wrap their baldness, but just like true queens, they took your rags and adorned themselves!"

Irma and her children moved into the Carolinas. Throughout the land, Irma could see the one named Christopher and his influence and death throughout the land enslaving masses of people of different races.

"Who was this vile human being that he should be judge, jury, and executioner?! I have seen his name several times before!" Irma bellowed as she continued to weaken.

"Mother, he influenced the sale of our brothers and sisters from your boundaries after he killed the indigenous people of these lands! Her children replied.

"My children knew about agriculture! They were stolen to make others fat off their backs! My children were brought here illegally within chains and stocks while the people of light shades could immigrate even as indentured servants! I will never forgive it! I will never rest in peace until every one of my children is returned to my soil!"

The children noticed something different in Irma.

"What is it mother, what is happening?" they asked.

"I am growing weary children," Irma said.

"These Carolinas are the last place I will try to find your brothers and sisters. My sister Jose is coming to help, but I might not be able to wait for her.

"But Mother," her children cried.

"Yes, children," She answered.

"We can hear our brothers and sisters crying throughout this land of almost three million square miles."

"I hear them, children," Irma answered.

"But there are boundaries that we cannot cross. My children came to the shorelines, and that is my destiny. I reached inland as far as I can go. I must go back into the ocean. I need these warm waters and the help of my children to guide and propel me. I am full and I must take you home for your final rest. Aren't you tired from this long journey?" Irma asked.

"Yes Mother, but we want to find them," they answered.

"So do I children, but there are some boundaries that we can never cross. Mother Africa will never stop looking. I don't think I will ever be able to retrieve my children from this land due to the boundaries of the shoreline but I am not sure. I couldn't find the ones on the islands either. I hear the cries of my children stronger than I did when I was traveling. This land is filled with hate and bigotry and the souls of my children can feel it. They cry out for mother to take them home. Because of the genocide of the people of this land, and carnage of those brought here against their will, there will be pestilence. There will be flooding on one side of the land while the rains will be held back as the other side burn in consuming fires. From heaven, precipitation will fall in such abundance that the top of the mountains to the bottom will turn white during the winter. It will look as if the cloud filled sky and ground are touching. Rivers will overflow and cities will turn into oceans. There are things coming that I am not allowed to mention. Now, children, it is time to go home. Let my sister have her way."

On September 13th, Irma went back to Mother Africa speaking briefly to her sister Jose before she left with her children where she could take them to their final resting place. When she got home, she told Mother Africa that she needed help because the people on the mainland of America were wailing in prayer and the outcry of slaves in the soil was so great.

CHAPTER 5

Jose

As hurricane Irma began to fill up, she summoned help from the continent of Africa because she could not find her children and she was tired.

Just as Irma had done, Mother Africa began to prepare for another voyage. She began to develop on September 5th, 2017. The only way that she could make the long journey was to increase in strength. On September 6th, 2017, Mother Africa became Hurricane Jose. She picked up her children from the ocean, continued to pick up strength and speed, reaching one hundred and fifty-five miles per hour quickly. The Caribbean chain of islands was in fear that another hurricane was about to hit the same islands that were already devastated by Hurricane Irma.

Everyone in the Caribbean and the worldwide Caribbean diaspora held their breaths and waited. Jose, just like her sister, Irma, had picked up the spirit of her children from the ocean but this mission was different. Though she became a Category 4 Hurricane, she was trying to see what her sister needed.

The people of Antigua and Barbuda had begun to prepare before Irma came. Two days after Hurricane Irma passed the sister islands, hurricane Jose became a second threat. Jose added fear to the already frayed nerves of the people left on the Island of Barbuda.

The remaining inhabitants thought better than to stay on the island. Although their sister island of Antigua sustained some damage, it was not as bad as Barbuda. An evacuation was ordered, and for the first time in its three-hundred-year history, Barbuda was left uninhabited. Only the stray animals and livestock were left to walk the streets and tell the story. Fortunately, Jose moved forty- five miles Northwest of the island and back into the Atlantic.

Her children guided her in that direction and reminded Jose that her purpose was to see what Irma needed. Jose watched from afar at what her sister Irma had done. The children inside of her cloud held her eye open and were horrified to see the devastation to the islands. The children saw islands scrubbed clean of their vegetation. Lands of lush green vegetation had been turned to a dull brown with the landscape looking like a shorn bald head that was left patchy. There was destroyed infrastructures, livestock, and human loss. They saw how Irma had destroyed their means of transportation and the islands means of income of tourism. Some buildings had been demolished to the foundation like they had never been built as Irma's winds took back what she felt the need to remove. Since Jose had not picked up as many children as her sister had, on September 11th, 2017, Jose began to weaken.

Jose could feel the energy of her sister Irma. She became stuck due to the force of Irma's circulation. There was no way to get closer to her. Jose began to slow down to figure out how to avoid Irma's circulation.

The children Jose picked up in the Atlantic told her to make a loop over the Atlantic and wait for Irma to speak.

L. A. DAVIS

As Jose sat off the coast of Massachusetts, she saw how the indigenous people were enslaved before Africans touched the shore. They were so despised that they were traded for Africans in the Caribbean. Jose called out to her children as she sat in the ocean. They entered her cloud of peace as they were greeted by their brothers and sisters.

"How did you get here?!" Jose asked.

"We all jumped, Mother."

"Why did you jump into the ocean?" Jose asked.

"We were afraid of those men. We had never seen men with such fair skin. They threatened to lash and shoot us if we didn't do what they said. We couldn't always understand them, so they motioned to us. A few of them spoke our tongue. We were always being beaten. We stayed on the ocean for so long that we thought we would never see land again. We didn't know where we were going. One day we heard the slave masters talking. They said we were going to live with strange people. I shared the information with others on the ship. Hundreds of us planned this because we didn't want to be separated. When we finally saw the land, we held hands and jumped. Some jumped because the slave masters got angry at them since so many of us jumped. We were making them lose money and the other slaves were scared of being beaten because of it."

"All of you jumped into the ocean?!" Jose asked again.

"Yes Mother, we did; we knew that we would find our way back to you one day."

The thought of her children drowning made Jose stir the sea with anger!

"Where are my children?!" Jose cried out as she slammed tons of water against the coast! As she screamed, her cloud began to fill up with more children.

WHERE ARE MY CHILDREN?!

"We are here, Mother! We lept into the sea from ships. Many of our sisters and brothers did not leap with us, and they are beneath the soil in these lands." Her children replied.

"Are you talking about the ones on land? They will not come to me!" Jose cried.

"They are in the soil mother," her children replied.

Jose and her children watched as the big-bellied beasts of the sea carried provisions for sale along with human cargo.

"Mother look at that," her children within her cloud cried. She sat back in the Atlantic waiting for her sister to tell her what she needed as she continued to drive her winds and rain on the coast eroding much of the shoreline there.

"All along the coast of this place called New England our brothers and sisters were deposited from your shores." Her children lamented.

"I see them, children," Jose answered.

"Some of my children were so weak that they could not be sold for any value! All along this coast, I see this happening! They swelled their population off the backs of my children!

"Who is this one by the name of Emerson, Children?!" Jose asked.

"Mother, Emerson was a slave owner who traded us for fine spirits, fine drink, fine poultry, and butter. We were not allowed to touch any of it. He was a man of gluttony packing his ships so tightly that dysentery spread like lice amongst us. His descendant was a famous author who didn't share the same views."

Thousands of children within Jose's cloud cried!

"We died of that dreadful disease! We were starved for most of our journey here! We were fed food that was not fit to feed swine although the cellars were ripe for the picking. We became infected, and we had to lay in our body secretions.

We thrust from our stomachs until there was nothing, but bile left. As punishment for vomiting and releasing our waste, we were not given any water to quench our thirsty mouths, and it killed us. We died with gladness though we had to suffer to get to it. We wanted to come home to you. Thank you for finding us," they cried.

Jose was the second longest lasting hurricane. She lasted twenty days. She and her children moved back and forth on the upper east coast as they watched slave owners turn away slaves that were too old to work.

"After my children were too old to work, you turned them out onto the streets! You had to be forced to keep them, and you still mistreated them out of your resentment! They were not a burden, they were human, and they were my children! My children served you, and you took their children from them and gave them away when you didn't want to take care of them! You tore my children away from me and then you tore their children away from them! This place called Boston who purchased an abundance of my children did not allow them the freedom they deserved! They fell beneath the lash if they disobeyed your laws and to this day you show my descendants less respect that you show the dog! Just as you lashed them, I will lash your homes and your shores!"

Anger continued to fester within Jose.

"I will pour into you the fear that my children felt while inside the walls of those dirty ships!" she screamed.

WHERE ARE MY CHILDREN?!

"How dare you come to this land and spread your superiority over my children! Where are they!? Where did you hide them?! Give them back to me!

Jose continued to sit in the ocean, waiting for her sister Irma to speak. When she did, Irma told Jose thanks for coming but they needed more help. Irma explained that the cries of her children were more than she had ever heard, and she would be returning home to Mother Africa with her children and to ask for more help.

"What is that noise?" Jose asked Irma.

"It is the cries of our children and we can't get to them! I am full and weary, and I am returning home for rest," Irma replied.

"You go ahead sister, I will stay and continue to pick up more of my children until I am full," Jose said to Irma.

Jose continued picking up children from the ocean for twelve more days. She dissipated on September 25, 2017; days after her sister Maria made her grand entrance.

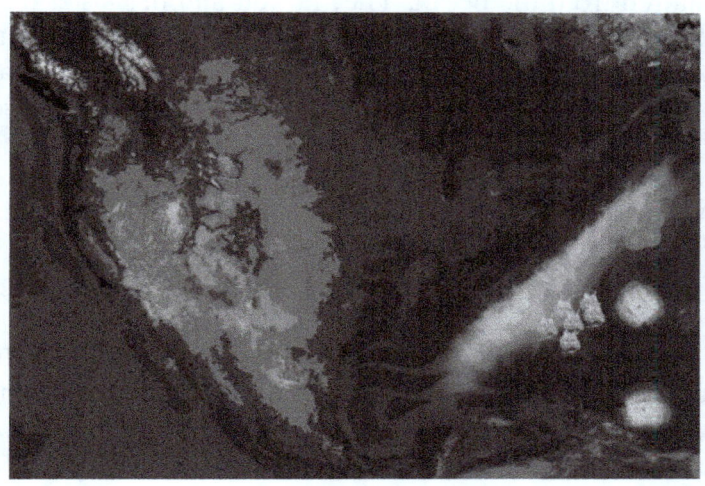

CHAPTER 6

Maria

On September 12th, 2017, after Irma returned to her sleep state, Mother Africa prepared for another trip. Her storm cloud developed six hundred miles away from Cabo Verde the same way her other sisters prepared for the journey. It took Mother Africa six days to prepare, but once she did, she was worse than her sisters. Within twenty-four hours on the 16th of September, Mother Africa developed from a tropical depression to a Category 4 Hurricane named Maria. Maria followed the path of the middle passage that her sisters Irma and Jose followed. Maria called out to her children from the ocean. They flowed into her faster than when the Irma and Jose called to them, causing her cloud to grow quickly. Just like Irma and Jose, her children began to form a circle with their backs to the cloud to form an eye.

"Thank you, children, for allowing me to be able to see."

"You are welcome mother." her children replied.

Maria asked her children, "Where did those ships take your sisters and brothers?"

"They went that way, Mother, towards the West" her children answered.

Maria went in the same direction that her sisters went, but she did not follow the exact path. Irma had traveled to different islands, but she was unable to find any children on land.

WHERE ARE MY CHILDREN?!

Maria and her children watched as crew members of slave ships picked up slaves from the Senegambia, Sierra Leone, Nigeria, Guinea, Cameroon, The Windward coast, Liberia, Ghana, Benin, Congo, and Angola. Maria was puzzled by this since the slave coast was broken down in such a way that other slave trade companies would stay within a specific area, yet these ships were all over the coast. She couldn't be bothered with that now. She had a mission to complete. Maria and her children within her cloud started to move. They watched as the ocean was dotted with ships like it was a freeway.

"Mother, look at that!" Her children said.

"Yes, children I see all of those ships traveling in one of three directions."

"Mother, some of them are so close together that they look like fleets of vessels going to the same destination." Her children cried.

Maria moved quickly to find her children who were crying out for help from the Americas. Her storm cloud roared as she moved. As she called out to her children from the depths of the sea, they continued to flow into her cloud of protection in large numbers.

My sister Irma told me that my children are crying for me. I am going to find them. Do you know which way those vessels traveling to the West took your brothers and sisters?"

The children replied, "Keep going West mother, we will tell you when to turn."

As Maria and her children began to travel over open water, more children flowed into her cloud as she called them from the abyss of the ocean. Maria watched as one ship had her male children on deck. Many of them had become seasick and were vomiting profusely. They could stay on deck for fresh air. Crew members did not want the extra hassle of vomit being added to the excrement and bodily fluids always present in the decks. Maria noticed that her children were wearing clothing. There wasn't much clothing, but at least they were covered.

"Hmmm," Maria said. "These vessels have more woman and children than men. I wonder why?"

While on deck, Maria and her children noticed crew members trying to force her male children to dance. Although dancing was considered a form of entertainment and exercise, Maria was furious at what she was seeing. Maria watched as her male children were unshackled and surrounded by crew members. There were no drumbeats, no tempo, no clapping of hands or stomping of feet, just crew members pointing on the deck floor, moving in mocking motion while they laughed. Those who did not dance were beaten severely with whips!

Maria screamed with fury.

"You beat my children with whips because they will not dance to your invisible music?! They do not refuse to dance out of defiance! They do not dance because they do not speak your tongue! They do not understand your commands!"

Maria became filled fury. She did not anticipate that she would see such visions while she traveled. She wondered if this is why her sister Irma needed her to make this trip. Mother Africa had never sent out such fury so quickly to this region. Maria didn't know what this was about. She only knew what she had to do.

WHERE ARE MY CHILDREN?!

As she traveled, her children yelled, "Mother, look! What is that!?"

Maria answered, "Do not look, children; they are your sisters and brother jumping into the abyss of the sea!"

Her children watched in horror as millions of white dots were splashing into the ocean. They cried out.

"Dear Mother! Some of us jumped and many of us who weren't strong enough to jump prayed to be thrown overboard. We felt it was the only way to return to you! We didn't know any better. We didn't know it would be so painful!"

"I told you not to look, children! she yelled.

"Your purpose is to propel me and guide me to where I can find your brothers and sisters!"

"Forgive us, it is different looking at things from this point of view. It is only now that I see how truly horrifying or tribulations were." her children cried.

"Please don't worry. Those who were buried in the cemetery of the ocean will forever be picked up because your bones were not returned to the soil. None of my sisters could pick up our children from the land," she replied.

WHERE ARE MY CHILDREN?!

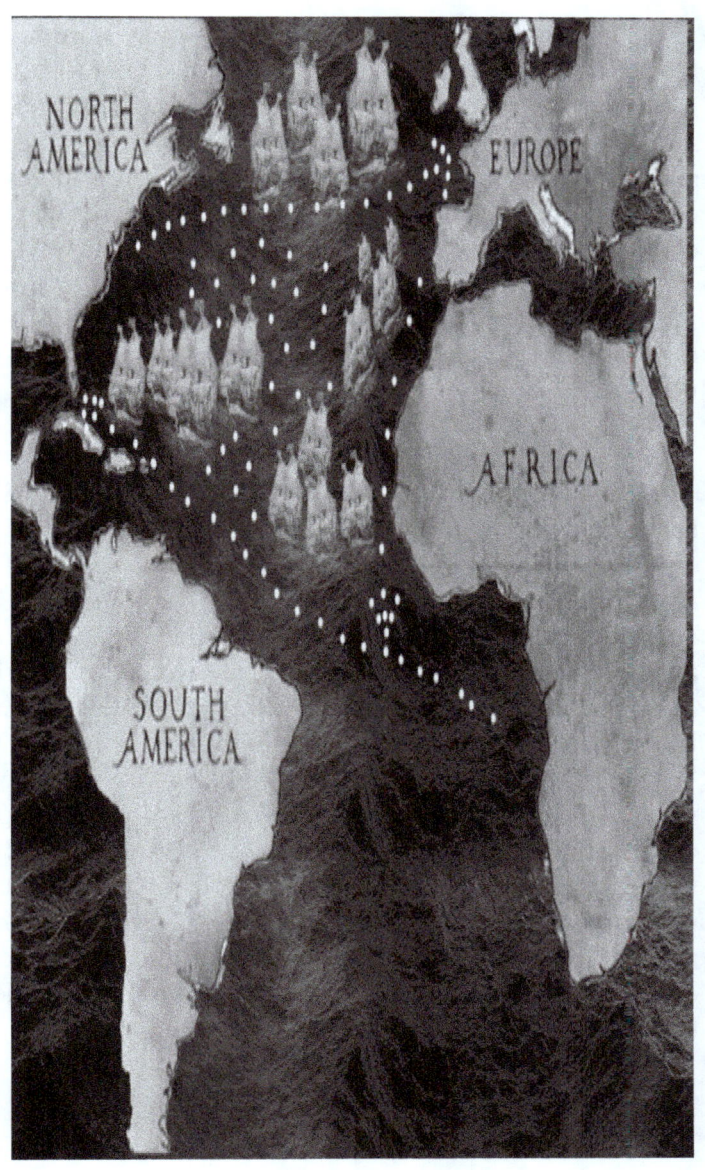

Maria and her children continued to grow and move as fast as she could go in the direction, they told her too. What Maria saw next was so horrifying that nothing Irma and Jose saw could compare. She watched as women who were torn away from their families and had become pregnant either through marriage, or rape of traders were preparing for childbirth.

Although slave traders preferred men over women, pregnant women brought extra money. If women could make the trek to the coast while pregnant, slave traders did not care.

"Mercy children!" Maria exclaimed.

"What is it mother?" they asked.

"Look only if you want too, this is really bad!" Maria replied.

Maria and her children watched as in the middle of the night hundreds of African women gave birth to their children in the holds. Slave ships held midwives that knew about child birthing, and women always came together. Even though many of the women did not speak the same language, they knew the pain of childbirth.

Scantily clad children of Mother Africa removed whatever clothing they could to provide a dry, clean space on the floor. Maria and her children watched as these women gave birth. The screaming and moaning of these women went uncared for by the crew or captain, yet Maria and her children could hear it. In several cases, the crew didn't know the child had been born until it was time to bring the women on the deck.

The men inside of the cloud were horrified and screamed so loudly that it sounded like thunder.

WHERE ARE MY CHILDREN?!

The women cried causing torrents of rain to pour from the cloud. Maria was beside herself with rage!

"Over the centuries, my children were forced to give birth in the stagnant filthy air of the hold! My children were used to birthing at home with a peaceful environment and drank herbs to decrease their pain! Many of my children lost their babies during the night because of these dark, hot, and dirty sea dungeons!"

Maria and her children watched as women were forced to wrap their babies in rags and throw them overboard! There were no sharks to tear them apart. The women stood on those ships and watched their babies float until they were out of sight! Maria had thousands of babies in her cloud that were brought up by her other children. Though the babies were with Maria, she saw that the mothers were never the same.

"You evil, wicked men!" Maria boomed!

"Mother! I don't think I can take this," her children cried.

"Do not watch whatever you cannot bear children!" Maria wept.

Maria and some of her children watched as many women who tried to give birth couldn't. Their babies had their cords wrapped around their necks and had become lodged in their birth canals. Some babies could not be delivered because the child tried to present in the wrong direction. Many of the skilled women tried as hard as they could to save the woman, but the tools needed were unavailable. All they could do was soothe the mother until she passed away in distress. Mother and baby would be thrown overboard like trash. On some ships, the crew allowed the slaves to give a decent sea burial. Thousands of

119

babies were stillborn due to the stress of the journey on their mothers. Many women miscarried.

Maria erupted in rage as she sped up and grew!

"You made my children who had given birth stay in the dirty holds with no one to care for them or their babies! They were hungry! They needed to be fed! While mothers were in those holds, it gave them time to think of things that a new mother should never be thinking about! They held their babies to their un-swollen breasts to suckle! The babies lacked milk because their mothers were malnourished! Those women could not quiet the cries of their children's tiny hungry bellies! They could not soothe their crying children! There was no clean place for a new mother and her baby to rest or heal! You forced them to take matters into their own hands!"

"Mother no!" her children shrieked!

All the children in the cloud including the men started crying at the terrifying scene. As soon as they found the opportunity, mothers held their babies, said a prayer, and jumped overboard. Maria and her children closed their eyes and shrieked in terror!

Maria did not think she could witness anything worse, but she did. As she continued to travel, she noticed on another ship that the strongest of her warriors were being violated. One night during a rebellion where the slaves were getting the upper hand, gunshots rang out. Maria watched as the order was restored to the ship. No one was whipped, yelled at, or thrown overboard. Slaves were settled back into the deep of the ships to contemplate and worry about what would happen.

The slave traders had a master plan. The next morning all the male slaves who were involved with the revolt were

WHERE ARE MY CHILDREN?!

brought up on deck in front of the other slaves. Some were frightened, and others were not. They had already lost everything, so what was there left to fear? The strongest of the group were shackled to the deck, and the other slaves involved in the revolts were forced to sexually defile them as the other slaves were forced to watch.

Those who refused to participate, or watch what was happening, were immediately killed and thrown overboard. All the female slaves huddled together in petrified fear and cried while the men puffed up in a rage that they could not release. After this act, none of the men involved in the rape was ever able to lift their eyes to look at anyone again. They succumbed to the ocean because their spirits had been utterly broken. There was no hope, and nothing left to live for. Hundreds of male children within Maria's cloud moaned.

"Forgive us, Mother, we leaped into the ocean because the day that vile act was cast on us, we were dead."

"Forgive us my brothers for defiling you! We were cowards. We would have rather died than to violate you like that, but we were afraid to fall beneath the bullet. We decided to jump because the guilt was too much."

Maria was so enraged that her cloud formed a waterspout with lightening shrieking through it and her eye began to shrink. Her children with their backs against the winds of her eye could no longer hold on. Some of them were squeezed back into her cloud as others fell out and had to be recaptured by Maria.

121

L. A. DAVIS

WHERE ARE MY CHILDREN?!

Maria was so angry that her eye shrank to only ten miles wide. As Maria and her children barreled towards the Caribbean, they finally saw land.

"Tell me which way you saw those sea creatures take your brothers and sisters!"

The children answered, "Go, Northwest, Mother."

Maria was guided to the island of Dominica.

Dominica

On September 18^{th,} at 9:00 p.m., Maria slammed into the island of Dominica affecting Guadeloupe and Martinique with unbridled fury. Wind speeds were one hundred and sixty miles per hour winds. She destroyed as many boats as she could.

"Where are my children?!" she howled.

"You slave traders were so greedy that you brought my children from all points of my land to work your fields! After landing here, you scattered them like seeds to other islands like Guadeloupe and Martinique! You wanted them to grow your goods to enrich your lives while leaving my children and their descendants in poverty! When my children remembered that they were from a place of brave warriors, they decided to take their freedom back from you! You punished them by planting sticks and placing their head on their pricks to frighten their brothers and sister! You placed their headless bodies on the gallows! Where did you hide the bones of my children?!"

Maria wasn't finished.

"You gave my children lashes until their blood flowed from their backs! You burdened them with heavy ropes of chains as punishment while they worked the land! You whipped my children until they fell to their deaths under the sounds of your whip! You didn't care if they were male or female, but I do! Even after their lashes, some of them you sold again! You forced my children to make you rich through agriculture! I will scrub this land clean to the dust! I will remove your existence this very day from this place! For this abomination, I will punish you! I will shake you until you are loosened from the earth! The French and British with their greed shall forever be in turmoil for this abomination!"

Dominica experienced the worst hurricane in its recorded history when Maria slammed into her leaving massive damage to her infrastructure. Over ninety percent of her structures received damage to their rooftops. The island sustained damage from intense flooding. Maria was not finished. While she pummeled Dominica, she also beat surrounding islands at the same time with punishing winds and ocean surges.

Martinique

On September 18th, while hurricane Maria blasted Dominica, she was also beating Martinique and Guadeloupe. She continued to call her children who flowed into her from the ocean. Maria and her children watched and scanned for their brothers and sisters who they could hear crying out from the land.

"Who is that mother?" her children asked.

"The man named Christopher is here! Children."

"We see him mother, what a wretched man he is!" they cried.

WHERE ARE MY CHILDREN?!

Maria and her children watched as the French brought their sisters and brothers to work this land. They were sent through the tunnel of death on those sea vessels to cultivate and harvest their white gold of salt. Maria was saddened by what she saw.

"My sisters centuries ago visited this place and dried up the sugar mills! They took more than two thousand of you for your wickedness! You created mandates against my children and then treated them as your property to sell as you chose! Where are my children?! What have you done with them?!"

"They cannot answer you, mother. We hear them crying, but they cannot answer because they are within the soil. They went back to where they came."

"They did not go back to where they came! They came from me, and that is where they should have gone to rest! I will shake these islands until everything is moved from its place. Give my children back to me right now!"

As Maria continued to howl, more of her children started swarming into her cloud increasing her size and her speed. She continued to scream.

"When my children tried to free themselves, you would not let them be! Where could they go?! They could not go from this place because you took their means away from them! They could not get on ships to return to me! You killed my children! Some you hung by breaking their necks and others struggled until they suffocated! Their bodies stiffened as they struggled for air! You didn't do it yourselves! You made their brothers and sisters kill them so that they could never forget and remain afraid of you! Many of them killed themselves because the guilt was too great! Some you whipped until their skin turned white! The earth shook because of what you did to them! Let me remind you of something! From this day until forever; anytime the earth shakes, remember me! It is to avenge the deaths of my children!"

Maria damaged thousands of home leaving islanders without electricity or water. Many islands were not so lucky.

Guadeloupe

Maria slammed into the island on September 18th; she was still angry about seeing mothers and babies jumping into the ocean in a means to get their souls back to her.

"Where are my children?!" she thundered.

"I came to collect their souls and their bones! I will till the soil until I find them! For almost three centuries after you stole my children from me, you kept them, and my descendants enslaved! You killed so many of my children that you had to keep coming back to my shores to meet your quotas! You gave my children a small taste of freedom while your country was fighting for its freedom elsewhere!"

Maria's winds continued to blow with fury!

"You put my children back into bondage, you hypocrites! Once my children were given their freedom, you did not abide by the law of the land! You had my children on this land of Martinique forced into battle to give them what was rightfully theirs; their freedom and many died because of it! Out of fear, you were terrified that you would not have anyone to work your plantations on land that did not belong to you! You slave traders and owners defiled the bodies of my female children producing children with them!"

A small break wasn't in the picture as Maria's anger rose.

WHERE ARE MY CHILDREN?!

"To spite my children and continue to keep them in bondage although you claim they were free, you deprived them of monetary wages! You gave them pieces of worthless coins that kept them bound to the life they wanted desperately to escape! You did not allow means for them to eat properly! You did not protect them from illness, and because of that, you caused the suffering of parents by them having to bury their own seed! For this Guadeloupe, I am going to make sure you feel the sting of my winds as you made my children feel the sting of the whips!"

Maria left the island of Guadeloupe devastated. She allowed the ocean to go outside of its boundaries flooding the island in low-lying areas. Electrical poles were left broken like match sticks. Her winds removed rooftops which folded like tin foil.

Maria asked the children again; "Which way did your brothers and sisters go with Irma? I was trying to find her, but she is already home. Jose is still in the Atlantic but there is no way for me to reach her. We must always stay miles apart." she told them.

"Mother, I don't think you should follow the exact path. We are going to the place of America but there is such an outcry from the land that I am not sure we will be able to hold them all."

Maria and her children could only hear the voices of her children from the ocean, but none would answer her on land. No matter what these hurricanes did, none of them could find their children buried in the soil.

"Mother, only some of your descendants of these lands exist. Some families were removed from existence due to the families being killed.

L. A. DAVIS

"Which way did your sisters and brothers go?!" Maria asked again.

"Mother, you must go Northwest."

"Are you sure children? I do not believe this is the way my sisters went!"

"They didn't, but this is the way that those ships went, and we can hear our sisters and brothers calling for you," the children answered.

"Well, that is the way that I will go." Maria went back into the ocean making a sharp turn toward the West. She headed toward the island of St. Croix.

United States Virgin Islands
(St. Croix)

On September 20th, between 1 am. and 3 a.m., Maria roared into St. Croix with the strongest side of her eyewall coming within miles of the island. Maria and her children continued to travel over open water, picking up more children who answered her call. When Maria got close to the island, she and her children watched as thousands of indigenous people fell from hard work and disease.

"You evil, lazy, colonizers! You worked the people to their deaths! You could persuade them to work through means of force, but you could not get your own to harvest your crops! How dare you take my children from within my borders to make you rich? I saw your vessels as they pulled into my shores! I watched as they traveled the highways of the seas to get here! I saw how you killed my children for sport! I saw how you evil Danish took my children from my shores! One of my sisters took your souls to the bottom of the sea to join my children in their despair! She wanted you

WHERE ARE MY CHILDREN?!

to see their fear and remove from you the joy of your spoils! Every one of her children that died that day is here with me to bring wrath on you! I am here to collect the souls of the ones you sold!"

What did you do with my children!? I will destroy your sea vessels this day!"

Maria demolished as much of the shoreline as she could.

"My children did not out number you on this land, yet you feared them! The fear did not come from their strength! The fear came from your guilt! You made them pick cotton until their hands turned the plant red! You created your spirits, and demon rum out of the sweat of their pores as they pressed your sugar canes. You bent their backs over for hours each day with your cutting instruments to harvest your tobacco which brought pleasure to many while my children cried in pain every night! You took my children to till your soil that they made fertile! They planted your money-making sugar cane! That evil plant took millions of my children to their ancestors!"

Maria's winds drove into houses angrily, blowing homes until she saw them shake.

"While you enjoyed your coffee and tea, you killed so many of my children that you had to constantly pick Mother Africa's shores clean to keep up with your greedy demands!

While others enjoyed their freedom, you kept my children in bondage! My sisters cursed you and dried up your sugar cane and your mills! They freed themselves because my sons and daughters knew their worth! They knew their value, and they knew they deserved better! My queens came together with their brothers and caused a great fire in this land; one of which you had never seen before! Many of my children died trying to gain their freedom because of your military power! After this land burned, you took more of my children and shot them like dogs in the street! You subjected others to hard labor for the rest of their lives! Even though many died fighting to gain their freedom, the fire was such that it forced you to set my children free! they put such fear in you that they will never have to do it again!"

St. Croix sustained massive damage from Maria, leaving the island without electricity for months. Many were left without shelter or roofing. Request for financial assistance fell on deaf ears from the mainland.

Puerto Rico

September 20th, 2017 at 6:15a.m. Maria steamed full speed ahead to Puerto Rico picking up more of her children as she continued.

"Mother! this land and the U.S. Virgin Islands are different from all of the other islands that we visited, why are we going back to these places? Haven't they suffered enough?"

"Yes children, I sense that my sister has visited this place as she did the U.S. Virgin Islands, and yes there is still great suffering in many of these lands," Maria replied.

"I am bringing a great tribulation in these places just like my sister did because they belong to the great land that has caused much sorrow to my children. The cries from these lands are great and much louder than any of the other islands even though some of these islands are smaller than some my sisters and I have visited. The cries and prayers are coming from these islands like a heavy drumbeat. I hear my children just like my sisters did, but they will not come to me because they can't. Like every other island, they are in the soil. People from America and abroad bring their attitudes and their norms from wherever they are from and expect my children to adapt to them on their own land! My children have been mistreated and disrespected on these islands! They are tired of it, and so am I! My children are tired of the corruption! they are tired of being taken advantage of and they are tired of being overlooked! They are a hard-working and resilient people who haven't received the respect they so justly deserve, and the day of reckoning is here! The attitude of this new administration has been slowly seeping into the veins of the people who live here from those who travel here, and from those who have settled here! The ancestors in the soil that are nothing but dust, called for Mother Africa to intervene! That is what I am here to do! On this island, the Spaniards desecrated this land just like the land belonging to the natives on the land of America and I am here to fix it!"

Maria destroyed the electrical grid on the island that left it in complete darkness for months. Some have still not gotten their electricity returned. Bridges disconnecting people from one part of the island to the other were destroyed. Patients in hospitals died as machines needed to keep them alive failed due to lack of electricity. Many were left without fresh water and food and yet Maria continued on her path.

Grand Turks and Caicos

September 22nd, 2017, Maria, and her children came ashore and watched in horror as her children by the thousands worked salt ponds. Her children raked salt for hours a day in the blazing sun. They watched as her children dropped dead in the fields where they worked, but there was something even worse and Maria thundered with fury.

"You put my children in the broiling sun with no rags to shield their heads! You made them stand with their bare feet on jagged salt crystals in the heated breeze of the Caribbean sun. Their blood seeped out of their feet because they were cut so deep! They endured the pain of salt entering their wounds!"

Maria watched as the legs of her children festered with boils from the saltwater pits.

"You wicked colonizers! You wicked slave owners! You had my children working these ponds with flesh that was eaten away from their bones! You didn't care that walking into the salt pits with water up to their knees with boils and blister filled legs was like putting a hot poker to wet skin! The sound of raking, water splashing, and shovel scraping was the only music they worked by daily because you beat the music out of them!

You made their weary bodies work late into the night with little time to rest! They were in agony! You didn't tend to their boils, and you gave them planks instead of sacks to sleep on! They were forced to make their beds the best way they could to bring relief! When my children could not keep up with the work pace due to their afflictions and racked bodies, you beat their skins until you broke it! You poured the very salt they plucked from the earth into their wounds and forced the other to watch as they screamed in pain! You devil's disciples! My children begged for death to relieve them so they could come back to me! I can hear them screaming, and for this, I will make you pay!"

WHERE ARE MY CHILDREN?!

Maria continued on her path screaming through her winds "Where Are my children?! Where have you buried them?!"

Maria's wrath brought down thunder, lightning, and rain as she called out to her children.

"Where did those ships go from here children?!"

"Mother, they went Northeast."

"Northeast," she repeated as she skirted by the Bahamas.

"Yes, Mother, this path is taking us to the mainland."

Her children in the cloud screamed! "We can feel and hear our sisters and brothers screaming for you all over that land mother!"

"I hear them too children," Maria replied. "I am full; I am tired as I have traveled a far journey."

Maria traveled raising the surf off the east coast of America. The children within Maria wept with great sorrow because they could not get to the mainland to find their brothers and sisters.

"Children listen to me," Maria exclaimed!

"I cannot go too far within the boundaries of that land. Islands are smaller; my sisters and I can cover them. I hear my children crying out in sorrow for me. It makes me very angry and full of sadness, but I realize something, and you must listen to me carefully before I take you home to Mother."

Maria explained calmly and sincerely to her children.

"My children, your brothers, and sisters who are in the soil, can never leave these lands. That is why when I and my sisters called to them, they would not come to us. They are here to watch over their descendants so that what happened to them will never happen again. We only came because our children called us. They needed us to stop what was happening because they knew things would get worse. If they leave these lands, their descendants will not be protected. If they are not here to cry out to Mother Africa, then worse atrocities are going to happen. You have seen within the last year how hate began to fill this world. It was not only in America but abroad also. It is traveling with the speed of a hurricane but unlike us, it can be stopped. Did you see what happened when we came? It caused a lot of monetary damage to America and it caused people to stop the fighting. Even if it was just temporarily, people were more focused on what we were doing. There is never a war without collateral damage and everyone who had a loss in this season was collateral damage. Many have fallen away from prayer; many have given up on believing in justice because innocent black men and women are being gunned down by those who should be protecting them. People are being attacked publicly because of the color of their skin, their religious beliefs, and their sexuality. Our planet is in great pain and she wants to work with us. While all of these issues are prevalent, some choose to look the other way while they live in luxury. My children are here in the soil all over the Americas to protect my children, your brothers and sisters, and all who are weary in spirit. They paid a very dear price, but in their deaths, they have found their purpose. If things do not change soon and my children begin to call on Mother Africa again, many of my sisters will continue to come. No one knows what they will see to make they grow in their strength, or which way their children will propel them."

Maria weakened to a tropical storm on September 28th and dissipated October 2nd, 2017, close to Ireland. The last of the fierce hurricane season went back to the continent of

WHERE ARE MY CHILDREN?!

Africa and into hibernation. Mother Africa has not forgotten the effects slavery had on its continent. In areas where men and women flourished, civilizations crashed leaving the continent open to colonization because there were not as many men left behind to protect and populate the continent. It caused a shift in the thinking of men who feel their race is more dominant than others. It created a change in the thought that men are better than women. In the days when Mother Africa was at her best, men and women worked in harmony to build civilizations. Men and women had their place with no one thinking they were better or less than the other. They knew their value and their role in society.

CHAPTER 7

Dust Clouds of Red

Irma, Jose, and Maria destroyed boats which they felt had brought their children to these shores. They inhibited travel by shutting down harbors, ports, and the ocean so others could experience what if felt like for slaves to be trapped with no way to get away when they were captured. They forced everyone to be stuck inside their homes so others could experience what slaves felt when they were stuck in buildings on the West Coast and when they couldn't go outside for days to weeks due to bad weather on slave ships.

They destroyed buildings and houses for us to experience how slaves felt when they had everything taken from them. They left everyone in darkness for weeks to experience what slaves had to endure while being held in dark forts, in the tween decks, and in the holds of slave ships. They cut off all means of communications to show us what slaves felt when they couldn't communicate with family and friends or when they didn't know what had become of them. They cut off all means of food supply and medical intervention for us to see how it felt when slaves had to go without food and had no access to medical care. They came to show us that we need each other just like slaves had to depend on strangers on slave ships to survive and to fight against the injustices of their captures.

WHERE ARE MY CHILDREN?!

We need to stay in prayer, no matter the religion. Irma, Jose, and Maria our Spanish sisters came to show us that we must stand up to injustice, and bigotry.

During hurricane seasons that are quiet, Mother Africa is still active in a different way. When Mother Africa needs rest, she sends out dust to remind us that she has not forgotten. In this annual event, the Sahara Desert blows dust that rides the waves of the trade winds through the middle passage. Millions of tons of dust hitch hike across the Atlantic and is deposited in the Americas.

It travels into the gulf stream settling in Texas, neighboring states, and the Amazon river basin where it gives much-needed nutrients to the Brazilian rain forest. Sahara dust fill beaches with sand in the Caribbean.

Depending on the amount of dust that travels, it helps to decrease the events of hurricanes, but it doesn't mean that Mother African is ignorant. No, she is like a sleeping volcano that puffs out smoke to make others aware that she is still here. She sends signs to represent that she has not forgotten the blood that was spilled out of her children.

When her dust blows into the warm waters of the Caribbean Sea and the Gulf of Mexico, it fertilizes algae causing bodies of water to turn red. When the sun sets, it gives the sun a dark orange to a red glow. When you see these signs, be grateful and know that Mother Africa is sleeping. When she is awake, her hurricane clouds of fury are coming.

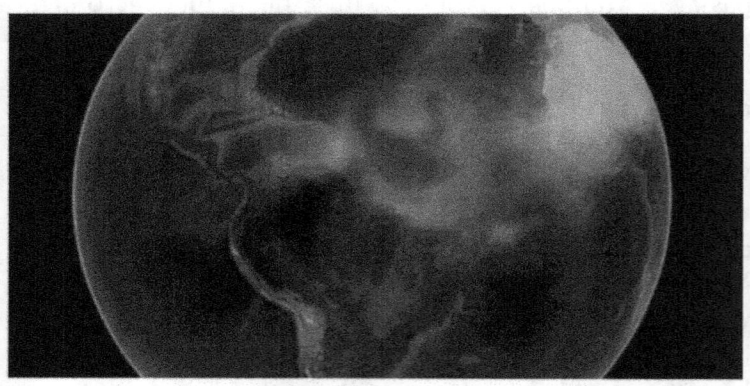

Conclusion

Hurricanes stretch the borders of the seashores and bring incredible amounts of damage. It is one of the scariest and most destructive weather phenomena. Unless you have been through one, it is hard to imagine. If you have been in a tornado, imagine it lasting hours or days instead of minutes. The wind howls, things bang against your boarded-up windows, and you hear explosions from power lines with rain that sounds like it is trying to destroy your roof to get inside. The calm may come temporarily as the eye pass over, then the worst part of the fury comes before the sun begins to shine again.

With all hurricanes, we hear about the devastation for a few months on television, on the internet and the radio. Eventually, another story comes and takes its place. People are left broken, with their worldly possessions gone. Some never see the sunshine again. They give up their hope, then their lives just to regain a sense of peace. Once the airwaves abandon the people that desperately need it, survivors of hurricanes are still left with the aftermath of these storms.

Cleanup is arduous with lack of emergency care, medication, food, and electricity making recovery more difficult. Dead livestock, mold, mildew, pestilence, infestations of anything that thrives on stagnant water find a fit home to cause plagues. Recovery may take years, and for some, it never comes. While we struggle to get our lives back to normal, nature comes back more beautiful than it was before.

We must respect nature, honor our planet, and protect her. If we do not, she will make it her business to do so. We must take care of our environment, our water supply, and our air. We must remember our history and hold on to it. African American and Black people are the only race of people who are told to get over past atrocities brought against us because slavery was so long ago. Why should we forget our past when other races and ethnicities commemorate their history yearly? Perhaps the fact that our ancestors are no longer around to give a fresh account is one reason. Perhaps the history is too painful for some to absorb or believe. It is a stark lesson to learn. Human beings can be incredibly evil to each other. Try as anyone might; there is no justification for it.

Our ancestors started crying out all over the land, and we should continue to listen. Those who forget the past are bound to repeat it, and there will be a very high price to pay. The racial injustices of the past will no longer be tolerated! Never forget the sacrifices made by any of those before us. It doesn't matter where you were born. We are all valuable.

The 2017 Hurricane season ended on Thursday, November 30th, the same day it ends every year. That year was the first year I had ever exhaled in relief. I still haven't taken that shot of wine followed by a chaser of wine. The experience left me with a new respect for nature and hurricanes. It gave me a new respect for the human spirit, and it allowed me to see my emotional limits.

I believe that hurricanes Irma, Jose, and Maria came to teach us all a valuable lesson and I hope we have all learned from them. Hurricane Irma caused one hundred billion dollars in damage taking one hundred and twenty-four souls with her. Hurricane Jose caused almost three million dollars' worth of damage and took one soul with her. Although Hurricane Maria hit fewer islands than Irma did, her path of destruction left over one hundred and two billion dollars in damage with a reported total of three thousand two hundred and one souls being lost with two thousand nine hundred and seventy-five soul lost on the island of Puerto Rico alone. May they all rest in power as they rest in paradise.

The End. For now!

L. A. DAVIS

Honorable Mentions

A brief history of the Danish West Indies 1666-1917.

Aboard a Slave Ship, 1829, (2000) Eyewitness to History.

African Enslaved: A Curriculum Unit on Comparative Slave Systems for grades 9-12.

African Heritage and Memories of Slavery in Brazil and the South Atlantic World.

African Societies and the Beginning of the Transatlantic Slave Trade.

Alexander Falconbridge's account of the Slave Trade.

An Account of the Middle Passage.

An Essay on the Slavery and Commerce of the Human Species, particularly the African

Atlantic Slave Trade.

Body positions of slaves in hold of French slave ships Aurore 1784.

Britain slavery and the trade in enslaved Africans.

Clement Lindley Wragge and the naming of weather disturbances.

Cinque the slave trader: Some new evidence on an old controversy.

Cowrie shells: Slavery and global trade.

European discovery and settlement.

First Hand accounts Case Study.

Five horrifying ways enslaved African men were sexually exploited and abused by their white masters.

Hell on Water: The Brutal misery of life on slave ships.

History of the slave trade in St. Barths.

History Revisited: Several heads of slaves in Dominica stuck on poles.

WHERE ARE MY CHILDREN?!

How African male slaves were raped during slavery- A bitter history.

Hurricane Barbara, 1953.

Hurricane Danny recap.

Hurricane Fred: Cape Verde's first hurricane in modern times:

Life on Slave Ships

Hurricane Irma.

Hurricane Irma: Facts, Damage, and Costs.

Hurricane Jose

Hurricane Maria.

Hurricane names: A brief (and sexist) history.

Hurricanes of the 1950 season.

Hurricane research division: Atlantic oceanographic and meteorological laboratory.

Laboratory Methods for the Diagnosis of Epidemic Dysentery and Cholera.

Middle passage black gold.

Minorities and Indigenous peoples.

National hurricane center.

National hurricane center.

Notes on the history of slavery in Massachusetts.

Resistance and Rebellion.

Resistance in Africa.

Slave ship mutinies.

Slave ships and slaving. Salem Massachusetts.

Slave ships and the Middle Passage.

Slave Trade: The African Connection, Ca 1788.

Slavery and the struggle for freedom in St. Martin.

Slavery in Massachusetts

Slavery in Zanzibar.

L. A. DAVIS

Ten facts about the Arab Enslavement of Black people not taught in school.

The Atlantic crossing.

The capture and sale of enslaved Africans. (2019).

The East African Slave Trade.

The fascinating history and evolution of Afro-Puerto Ricans.

The History of Mary Prince, A West Indian Slave Related by herself.

The Hurricane Washington: U.S.G.P.O.

The Memoirs of Alton Augustus Adams, Sr.: First Black Bandmaster of the United States Navy / Edition 1

The Middle passage.

The Middle Passage U.S. History Pre-Columbian to the new millennium.

The slave trade: Conditions on slave ships.

The Slave trade from the Windward Coast: The case of the Dutch 1740-1805.

The Triangular Slave Trade.

The Zong Case Study.

Wolfe, B. Slave Ships and the Middle Passage.

ABOUT THE AUTHOR

L. A. Davis earned her Doctor of Education with an Emphasis in Organizational Development in 2018 and her master's degree in Criminal Justice/Law in 2010. She discovered her love of writing after authoring her debut book *"So, You Want to Be A Doctoral Learner Huh? Are You Nuts?!"* which describes a story of triumph after a traumatizing experience with one of her chairpersons during her doctoral journey. She was born on the island of St. Thomas as is a member of Zeta Phi Beta Sorority, Incorporated. She is currently a dissertation coach with a specialization in qualitative methodology. *Where Are My Children?!* is her second book with more on the horizon.

https://thedissertationcafe.com

Contact Information

L. A. Davis
2403 W Stan Schlueter Loop #690923
Killeen, Texas 76549
Davislad2018@gmail.com

145

PRAISE FOR
THE FILES OF THE BSI

Omaha Stakes: "Action-packed.... Kal's frolic through a nifty supernatural world is enjoyable."
—Publishers Weekly

"*Chicago, The Windigo City* is jam packed with action but the heart of the story is Kal's love and concern for his girlfriend and his best friend .... An original and refreshing tale."
—Fresh Fiction

"*I Left My Haunt in San Francisco* is lively and smart. It is packed with action and just enough goop and gore to please fans of the genre without turning away newcomers to this subset of modern fantasy demon-busting.... It is just great, grand fun."
—ForeWord Reviews

What Happens in Vegas, Dies in Vegas: "A cracking good yarn from first to final page, no question.... Two very enthusiastic thumbs up for a job well and properly done."
—The Latinum Vault

Things to do in Denver When You're Un-Dead: "I have really enjoyed reading this book.... The story could just be one of guns, blood and guts and magic, but.... Mark Everett Stone has made these characters seem real."
—Fantasy Book Review

The Spirit in St. Louis: "A suspenseful dark fantasy saga. A balance between psychological intrigue, menacing chills and fierce resistance, The Spirit in St. Louis is a page-turner from cover to cover. Highly recommended!"
—Jack Mason (Mason's Bookshelf), Midwest Book Review

Other Books by
Mark Everett Stone

From the Files of the BSI
(Bureau of Supernatural Investigation)

Things to Do in Denver When You're Un-Dead
What Happens in Vegas Dies in Vegas
I Left My Haunt in San Francisco
Chicago, The Windigo City
Omaha Stakes
The Spirit in St. Louis
Talladega Nightmares

The Judas Line Chronicles

The Judas Line
The Judas Codex
The Judas Revelation